'You're planning to leave the State, just to *avoid* your family?' Tom said accusingly.

'See, I knew you wouldn't understand,' Jess responded.

'You're right, I don't. They're your *family*.'

'So? I didn't ask to be related to them, Tom. You don't know anything about the situation.'

'Tell me. What was your childhood like, Jessica? Was there never enough food to feed you and your siblings? Were all your clothes hand-me-downs that never quite fitted?' Tom's fingers were clenched tightly beneath the cover of his pockets.

'If you're going to start interrogating me then you can just forget any thoughts you might have about pursuing a relationship with me.'

'So what makes you think I want a relationship with you?'

'Are you blind? The attraction between us is impossible to miss!'

Lucy Clark began writing romance in her early teens and immediately knew she'd found her 'calling' in life. After working as a secretary in a busy teaching hospital, she turned her hand to writing medical romance. She currently lives in South Australia with her husband and two children. Lucy largely credits her writing success to the support of her husband, family and friends.

You can visit Lucy's website at www.lucyclark.net or e-mail her at lucyclark@optusnet.com.au.

Recent titles by the same author:

THE DOCTOR'S DILEMMA
THE FAMILY HE NEEDS
THE OUTBACK MATCH

EMERGENCY: DOCTOR IN NEED

BY
LUCY CLARK

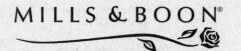

MILLS & BOON®

To my sister Kathy.
2Cor 5:16

First published in Great Britain 2002
Harlequin Mills & Boon Limited,
Eton House, 18-24 Paradise Road, Richmond, Surrey TW9 1SR

© Lucy Clark 2002

ISBN 0 263 83085 3

Set in Times Roman 10½ on 11 pt.
03-0802-52898

Printed and bound in Spain
by Litografia Rosés, S.A., Barcelona

CHAPTER ONE

'IS THE ambulance here?'

Jess heard the clipped tones of the deep, male voice before she saw the owner. A shiver of unease pricked its way down her spine as she listened to the footsteps drawing nearer.

'It's just pulling into the emergency bay outside, Doctor,' a woman's voice replied.

Within an instant, a tall man with short, dark hair and the most amazing blue eyes Jess had ever seen appeared in the doorway to the doctors' tearoom.

Jess's heart rate increased at the sight of her new boss and she wondered whether it was due to her apprehension of meeting him…or something else. Thomas Andrew Bryant. What she'd been told since she'd started two weeks ago at the Children's hospital in Adelaide *definitely* did him justice. She'd been told that although he was *the* most gorgeous man alive, he had a disposition, bordering on dismissiveness. Yet a lot of people agreed that he was brilliant with the children. It made Jess more curious about him— to say the least.

As his gaze scanned the room, Jess noted that although his eye colour was appealing his dissatisfaction with all he surveyed couldn't be contained. Forcing her apprehension about this meeting aside, Jess gulped down the rest of her coffee and stood.

His gaze settled on her. 'I take it you're Jessica Yeoman.'

What was that she heard in his tone? Objection? Disappointment? Jess reined in the flare of annoyance she felt at his words and squared her shoulders with determination. 'Correct.'

He looked her up and down, his gaze meeting hers for an instant, and Jess's indignation grew. He might be the director of the accident and emergency department but he still had no right to be so…so…insulting in his manner!

He raised one eyebrow, obviously reading her body language. 'You're taller than I'd expected. Ambulance is here. Let's go.'

And that was that, Jess thought as she followed him down the corridor to triage room one, which was kept specifically for emergencies. It didn't matter what she thought of Tom Bryant and his strange remarks about her height. The fact of the matter was that she had to work with him for the next six months—and work closely as she was his senior registrar.

For the moment, though, she had to concentrate on the job at hand, which was, as Belinda, the triage sister, had reported, a girl of ten who'd been involved in a motor vehicle accident.

Jess went to the sink and washed her hands before pulling on a pair of gloves as she heard the paramedic stretcher being wheeled in their direction. She closed her eyes for a second and took a deep breath. Focus. She exhaled slowly—wiping every diversion from her mind.

'You might work better with your eyes open, Jessica,' a deep voice said over her shoulder, and her eyes snapped open. She worked hard to control the unwanted response to Tom Bryant's nearness as she turned to look at him.

'Thanks for the tip,' she replied, her face deadpan. The paramedics appeared with their patient, the child looking very small on such a large bed.

The A and E staff burst into action, each person doing the job they'd been assigned. 'Patient's name is Ingrid Johansen,' the scribe nurse told the room as they got ready to transfer the patient from the paramedic stretcher to a hospital barouche.

'On three. One, two, three…lift,' Tom instructed as they

moved the small patient, who already had IV lines and monitors attached. The information relating to the patient was written on a whiteboard so all personnel could see it. 'Aged ten. Passenger in a motor vehicle accident with possible fractured right tib and fib, right radius and ulna, possible head injury due to temporary loss of consciousness at accident site. No analgesics administered.'

While all of this was being reported, the staff were working efficiently together, just like a well-oiled piece of machinery. Ingrid's clothes were removed while another member attached ECG leads as well as an oximeter.

Jess leaned over the small patient. 'Ingrid? Can you hear me?' There was no response and Jess checked her patient's pupils. 'Pupils equal and reacting to light but slightly sluggish,' she reported, knowing the information would be noted.

She continued with her assessment on the Glasgow coma scale, determined by Ingrid's responses to stimulation. 'Can you hear me?' Jess's voice was firm yet calm, and this time Ingrid stirred. Her eyelids slowly opened and she tried to speak.

'It's all right, Ingrid,' Jess reassured. 'Do you know where you are?'

'I can't move,' the child mumbled, her lips barely moving.

'You have a brace around your neck to keep your head still,' Tom said gently. Jess glanced at him quickly, taking in his soothing tone. At least he had a good bedside manner. 'Do you remember what happened?' he asked as Jess continued with her observations.

'N-no,' Ingrid replied, her tone wobbly with fright. 'I'm…sore.'

'I know,' he said calmingly. 'I'll fix that right now for you.' He turned to Jess. 'Morphine, stat.'

Jess authorised the request and the analgesic drug was checked by two nurses before they drew up the shot and administered it through the IV line. Jess knew it would start working almost immediately and their young patient would rest more easily.

Jess returned to checking Ingrid's injuries. 'She'll need X-rays of the right leg and right arm. I think we should do a CT as well.'

Tom had moved to the end of the barouche to check for Babinski's sign by firmly stroking the sole of Ingrid's feet with the stick end of a reflex hammer. The toes on both feet curled, indicating no damage to the motor system above the level of the spinal nerves. He reported his findings.

'Has she voided?' Jess asked the scribe nurse as she crossed around to Ingrid's left side.

'No mention of it so far.'

'The morphine's kicked in. She's sleeping,' Jess reported, and checked the ECG printout.

'Bladder rupture?' Tom queried, looking directly at Jess.

'Possible.'

'Call Urology as well as Ortho and have them send someone down,' Tom instructed the scout nurse. He crossed to the ECG machine and read the printout. 'Good. Neurological obs?'

The nurses called out their findings.

'Cross-type and match blood,' he ordered.

Jess attended to the gash on Ingrid's left thigh, which would require sutures. The intern had already given a local anaesthetic on Tom's earlier instructions, so when she removed the bandage Jess could clean it up before starting on the needlework.

'Neat stitching,' Tom remarked quietly over her shoulder. Jess didn't reply. She had no idea whether he was serious or teasing and she didn't have the time to find out. His comment also made her feel as though she were on trial.

Which, she reflected, she probably was. As this was the

first time Tom had seen her work, it was only right that he should want to know what his senior registrar was capable of. He'd been away at a conference for the past two weeks so, although Jess had worked with the rest of the A and E staff during that time, this was her first day with Tom.

By the time she'd finished her suturing, Nicola Muir, the urology registrar, had arrived and was giving her assessment of Ingrid's situation. The young girl stirred again and Tom was instantly back by her side.

'Hi, there, Ingrid. Do you know where you are?' He started the questions all over again and this time she remembered she'd been involved in a car accident. With tears in her eyes, she asked where her parents were. A lump formed in Jess's throat and she waited for Tom's answer.

'They're at Adelaide General Hospital.' Tom's tone was soothing and he pushed a lock of hair back from Ingrid's forehead. 'We've called your grandma and she's coming right in. Your mum and dad are getting help. I'll find out what's happening and let you know. Promise.'

This seemed to ease Ingrid somewhat and she closed her eyes again. 'That's a good girl,' Tom continued. 'Rest your body. We'll take good care of you.' It wasn't long before the orthopaedic registrar came in and soon Ingrid was being wheeled away for X-rays.

The next hour was filled with minor cases. When Ingrid's grandmother arrived, Tom and Jess told her what had happened.

'She's scheduled for surgery in the next ten minutes,' Jess said.

'Why don't you take Mrs Johansen to ESS where she can speak with the urology registrar,' Tom suggested, and Jess agreed.

'What is this ESS?' Mrs Johansen asked as Jess led the way out of Tom's office.

'It stands for Emergency Surgical Suite. It's the emergency operating theatres. As Dr Bryant explained, the scans have shown that Ingrid's bladder was ruptured in the accident so the urology registrar will repair that before the orthopaedic registrar takes over to fix her broken bones.' Jess slowed her step and pointed to a small waiting room. 'If you'll wait in here, I'll get the urology and orthopaedic registrars for you. Can I get you a cup of tea or coffee?' she asked, gesturing to the refreshments on the bench.

Mrs Johansen shook her head. 'Will there be anything I will be needing to sign?'

'Yes. As Ingrid's next of kin, once both registrars have explained the operation to you, they'll ask you to sign a consent form.'

'And my son and his wife? When do I hear more of them?'

Jess smiled. 'I'll have someone contact Adelaide General for an update. Have a seat and I'll track down the registrars for you.' Jess continued down the corridor and pushed open the swinging doors into the restricted area.

'Hi, Jess,' The urology registrar greeted her.

'Hi, Nicola. I've put Ingrid Johansen's grandmother in the ESS waiting room for you to explain the operation.'

'Thanks. I'll get Dirk and we can see her together.'

'Might be easier that way.' Jess tried not to grimace at the mention of the orthopaedic registrar. Dirk Robertson had asked her out on her first day at work and hadn't taken her refusal seriously. Every time she'd seen him, he'd smiled wolfishly at her and asked her out again. 'I'd best get back.' Jess glanced around nervously.

'Yes. With Tom back on deck, you're probably wise.'

Jess hurried back towards A and E without running into Dirk. She sighed with relief when she reached the sanctuary of the triage area. The last thing she'd felt like right at that moment was fending off another one of Dirk's advances.

'That's a heavy sigh, Jessica.'

Jess turned to see Tom leaning against the doorframe to a cubicle, eyeing her closely.

'First I catch you closing your eyes and now sighing. I sincerely hope you're not going to fall asleep any time soon.' His tone was dry and his expression bland.

Jess bit her tongue—literally—forcing herself not to say the first thing that came into her head. Tom was her boss and, even though she might not appreciate his attitude, she still had to work with him. Indeed, he'd been marvellous with Ingrid, setting their young patient at ease during her time in Radiology and before she'd headed off for her pre-med.

'I'll try not to,' she replied, her own tone equally as bland.

Tom's gaze narrowed slightly. His new senior registrar was being awfully cool towards him and he wondered if she'd been listening to the rumours about him. He decided to test her to see what type of person she was. 'Is hospital gossip accurate?'

'Why do you ask?'

'Your air of indifference towards me is testimony to it.'

'Indifference?' Jess shook her head at his arrogance. 'So you believe that hospital gossip pertains only to you?'

Tom quickly hid his smile. Oh, she was sharp all right. 'That wasn't what I meant—and you know it.'

'Dr Bryant,' she said indulgently. 'If you'd like to know my opinion of you, just ask.'

Tom chuckled, pleased with her directness.

Jess felt his laughter settle over her like a warm blanket. It was a sensation she wasn't sure she wanted—not with her boss.

'All right, then,' he continued, happy to play along. 'Tell me, Jessica, what's your opinion of me?'

Jess raised her eyebrows. 'You expect me to make up my mind after only a few hours of your acquaintance?'

'Why not? When a patient comes in, you don't take several days to diagnose them.'

'Their diagnosis is a lot more cut and dried than this.'

Tom edged a bit closer towards her and his tone dropped a few decibels. 'So is there something we need to diagnose?' He watched as her eyes opened wider in astonishment. Damned if he wasn't flirting with her! The knowledge surprised him as much as it surprised his new senior registrar.

He was flirting with her, Jessica realised. Thomas Bryant, who the hospital declared had a temper to match that of a Tasmanian devil, was flirting with her! The worst thing was…Jess found she liked him like this.

'Dr Bry-ant.' Her voice broke and she cleared her throat again, furious with herself for letting him see that his close proximity was affecting her. She took a small step backwards. 'Dr Bryant,' she said again, hoping to instil an icy calmness to her tone. 'The only condition I can diagnosis right now is one of annoyance.'

'Then at least I'm running true to form.' His gaze held hers. 'As far as I can recall, most of the staff find me annoying.'

'No. No, I believe the "a" word used to describe you was arrogant,' Jess countered.

'Aha! So you *have* been listening to the gossip.'

'Sometimes it's a bit hard not to. The point is whether or not I take any notice of it.'

'Fair enough.' He nodded, his lips tugging into a small smile. 'I'm glad we had this little chat.' With that he turned on his heel. 'I'll be in my office.'

Jess watched him go with a sense of increasing puzzlement. Had he just been testing her? It had certainly felt that way. Forcing all thoughts of Tom Bryant and the emotions he'd stirred within her to the back of her mind, she spoke to Belinda about getting someone to update Mrs Johansen on the condition of her son and daughter-in-law. Next, she headed to the nurses' station, which was situated in the centre of fourteen A and E cubicles, to see what other patients awaited her attention.

There was a steady stream of injuries and ailments, most of which were sorted out with little fuss. After lunch, which she finished eating just before two o'clock, she received a page from Tom's secretary asking her to meet him at three that afternoon. Jess made a note of it in her small pocket diary, wondering why he needed to see her.

'Jess?' Belinda called, and Jess went over to her. 'I've just received a call from one of the local schools to say that a child fell off a swing and cut his head. They're bringing him in now.'

'Ambulance?'

'Yes.'

'Right.' Jess looked out at the waiting room which was, for the moment, bare.

'I'll put him in triage two,' Belinda told her.

'Good. I'll just organise some equipment.' Within minutes, a boy of seven was brought through. There was dried blood streaked down one side of his face, making the injury look worse than it probably was. One of the paramedics was holding a pad of gauze, which was almost soaked, to the boy's head. Amazingly enough, the child wasn't crying. Instead, he was looking with interest at everything he saw. 'I'm Dr Jess,' she said to the boy. 'What's your name?'

'Robbie.' He gazed around the room with interest.

'Just try and keep still for a moment, Robbie. I hear you fell off a swing?' She took over from the paramedic. One of the nurses came in to assist her.

'Yep. Wow. What's that thing over there?' Robbie pointed and Jess quickly glanced across.

'That's a special light that I can move to where I need it to be.' Robbie turned his head to the other side and Jess held up her gloved hands for a moment.

'What's that?'

'Just hold still for a moment, Robbie,' she said again. 'I need to take a good look at this cut on your head.' There was always a lot of blood with head injuries—usually more than was warranted for the alarm they evoked.

'Do I need to have an operation?' Robbie asked, his tone excited. Jess almost laughed.

'No, but you'll probably need stitches—if you'll keep your head still long enough for me to have a proper look,' she chastised softly, a smile lighting her face.

'Uh, sorry,' he murmured, and tried to sit still. Jess could tell by Robbie's responses that he wasn't suffering from any neurological symptoms, and the nurse's observations confirmed it. She managed to find the source of the bleeding and began to prep the area ready for suturing. It was almost a relief when Robbie was drowsy from the midazolam as there was actually more than ten minutes of peace and quiet in the small room.

By the time his mother arrived, Robbie was back to fine form.

'Hi, Mum,' he said with enthusiasm. 'I've got *stitches* in my head,' he said as though it were a crown of gold.

'Really?' his mother asked, and gave her son a kiss. 'How has he been?' she asked Jess, as her gaze roved over every inch of her son, as though she was checking that he was really all right.

'Talkative,' Jess replied with a laugh.

'That's Robbie,' his mother responded with a sigh. 'He's always been very inquisitive.'

'Well, right now,' Jess said, 'I think we need to take an X-ray of that inquisitive head of yours to make sure you haven't done any other damage.'

'Cool,' Robbie replied. Jess wrote out the X-ray request form and waved goodbye as Robbie, thrilled with the prospect of a wheelchair ride, was wheeled away by an orderly. Jess wrote up his notes and smiled to herself. It was rare that she had patients such as Robbie and his laid-back attitude reminded her of her brother Scott. Jess felt a lump form in her throat at the thought of her brother. She still missed him so much. Deciding that now wasn't the time, she finished with the notes.

Jess checked the clock and said to Belinda, 'I'm due to have a meeting with Tom in five minutes so if you need me, you'll know where to find me. I'll be back to check Robbie's X-rays.'

'Sure. Good luck,' Belinda ventured.

'Will I need it?'

The triage sister shrugged. 'All I can tell you about Thomas Bryant is that he prefers children to adults any day.'

Jess hadn't heard that one before.

'I have no idea why,' Belinda continued. 'He's fantastic with his young patients, though, and I guess that's what counts.'

'I'd better hustle. I don't want to be late.' Jess walked out of A and E down the rear corridor towards Tom's office. His secretary sat in an outer office, with Tom's door directly behind her.

'Hello, Jess,' she said. 'He's just on the phone at the moment but he said to go right in.'

Jess swallowed, wondering why she was feeling suddenly nervous. She tapped softly on the closed door before opening it and walking through. He sat at his desk with the back of the chair facing the door, the phone cord stretched. Jess wasn't sure whether to close the door or not. Did Tom know she was here?

'I'm sick and tired of getting registrars who not only waste my time but the rest of the hospital's as well,' Tom said into the receiver. His tone held a hint of annoyance and Jess's eyes widened at his words. Was he planning on getting rid of her already? He'd only worked with her for a few hours. How could he possibly have made up his mind so quickly? Perhaps she should clear her throat, make her presence known.

'I'm glad you agree. Let me know what you plan to do.'

With that, he swivelled in his chair and replaced the receiver on its cradle. He glanced up at her and froze momentarily before saying, 'Well? Close the door and sit down.'

Jess did as he suggested, feeling even more unsure about working with him than she had before. She smoothed her hands down the top of her navy trousers before folding her arms across her chest, the stethoscope that was slung around her neck clicking as she did so.

'So how's your fortnight been?'

Jess was mildly surprised at the question. 'Ah…the fortnight. It's been fine,' she said, trying not to frown.

'The purpose of this meeting is to lay down the ground rules for the next two weeks and five months that you'll be working with me.'

Jess was stunned. Was he counting down the days already?

'Naturally, I expect punctuality and for you to always give your best to the patients. If you have any weak areas, I'd rather know about them now so I can compensate as well as assist you to improve them.'

Jess bristled at his words and clenched her jaw. 'I don't have any weak areas, Dr Bryant.'

'Am I the only colleague you call by their surname?' He paused for a second but Jess was still fuming from his last question. 'That's a bit ridiculous,' he continued when she didn't respond. 'You should know by now that this hospital adopts an informal policy, mainly because it helps relax the children. So, *Jessica*, you have no deficiencies? I'm glad to hear it. After all…' he looked down at the open file in front of him '…in two weeks and five months you'll be a qualified consultant. No more registrar status for you. It's good, very good to hear you have no weaknesses.'

Jess cleared her throat. 'I have no weaknesses, *Thomas*, because I think that's an extremely negative way of looking at things. I may have areas that require strengthening and

I sincerely hope that, as my boss, you'll guide me through them—so that one day I may be as perfect as you,' she finished. As the words she'd just spoken penetrated her mind, she clapped a hand over her mouth in horror.

'That's more like it,' Tom said as he leaned back in his chair, a smile on his face. 'Don't hold back, Jessica. Speak your mind.' So many adults hid their true feelings, their true agendas. Tom had little tolerance for such people. Honesty was a quality he liked in people and obviously Jessica had it in spades!

Slowly Jess removed her hand and stared at him. His features were so completely different when he smiled. She could lose herself in those eyes and the knowledge momentarily shocked her. She frowned at him.

'Don't stop now,' he prompted.

'Why?' Jessica hardened her heart against the unwanted feelings of attraction. 'S-so you'd have further grounds to fire me?' She gritted her teeth, cross with herself for stuttering.

'Fire you?' It was Tom's turn to frown. 'Why would I fire you? From what I've read in your file, you're an excellent doctor with a bright future ahead of you.' His gaze locked with hers, all pretence gone. 'Why would you think I wanted to fire you?'

'I heard you.' Jess pointed to the phone on his desk. 'When I came in just now, you were saying that you were sick and tired of registrars wasting your time.'

'And have you wasted my time today?' Again his tone was genuine.

'Uh…' Jess's hand dropped back to her lap. 'No. At least, not that I can recall.'

'Good. Then we understand each other. Plain speaking and don't waste my time.'

'As well as being punctual and giving my best to the patients,' she added.

Tom chuckled and the sight of his blue eyes twinkling

in merriment made Jess realise just how handsome he really was. A wave of goose-bumps spread over her body and she shivered involuntarily. She gave herself a mental shake and glanced down at her hands before looking at him once more.

'Perhaps the next two weeks and five months aren't going to be so bad after all. So tell me, Jessica, where are you planning to head to after you qualify?'

'I have a few places in mind but I haven't settled on any just yet.'

'Don't leave it too long. The rest of your training will fly by, especially with your main oral exam still to come.' He paused for a moment before saying, 'If you find you need some help with mock tests, please, let me know. I'd be only too happy to help.'

Jess had felt a multitude of emotions since she'd entered his office and now she could add surprise to the list. From the gossip she'd heard, Tom Bryant didn't put himself out for anyone except his patients and his department. Jess might be his registrar but were she to fail, it would mean nothing to him. He wasn't in the slightest way connected with her training, other than to write a report at the end of her time in his department.

It also drove the point home that hospital gossip could never be relied upon.

Tom stood and held his hand out to her. His gaze only had to dip a fraction to meet hers. How tall was she? Six feet at least. 'Welcome aboard, Jessica.'

Jess followed suit and placed her hand in his. He grasped it firmly and she was glad he didn't sport a limp handshake. Instead, his warm hand sent a jolt of tingles surging up her arm before they burst throughout her body.

Jess snatched her hand back as though burnt, all previous camaraderie gone. She glared at him with a mixture of surprise and shock, her breath catching in her throat. She need not have worried about Tom's reaction to her jerky movements because he seemed to be staring back at her with the same incredulous expression on his face.

CHAPTER TWO

JESS'S pager sounded and they both broke eye contact at the same moment. Tom cleared his throat and sat back down behind his desk. He glanced up at her as she checked the number on her pager.

'I guess that means my patient is back from Radiology.'

'Anything serious?'

'No. He just split his head open and I wanted a check X-ray to make sure nothing else is broken.' She paused for a moment and tilted her head to the side, smiling slightly. 'An amazing child, really. He was more interested in what was going on around him than belly-aching and crying while I attended to him. Quite amazing.'

Tom felt as though he'd just been kicked in the solar plexus. The way her shoulder-length auburn hair swished slightly and her green eyes sparkled made him catch his breath. She was a beautiful woman and, although he'd met many in his time, none had stirred him so immediately as Jessica Yeoman had.

She shook her head as though she was recollecting just who she was with. 'Uh…I'd better go before I'm paged again.' She crossed to the door and Tom admired her long legs.

Whoa! Slow down, he cautioned himself. He cleared his throat again and she paused in the open doorway, looking back at him.

'I presume you'll be admitting him to the neurosurgical ward for observation?' Tom couldn't stop his tone from coming out brisk.

Jess frowned and he knew instantly that he'd annoyed her again. 'Of course,' she stated as though she felt insulted. With that, she continued out of his office, closing the door behind her.

'Way to go, Bryant.' Tom leaned back in his chair and closed his eyes. He was still trying to come to terms with his unaccountable reaction to Jessica. From the first instant he'd seen her that morning, Tom had felt an unmistakable urge to make a favourable impression on her.

'Ridiculous,' he mumbled. Why should he care what she thought? Sure, she was beautiful and intelligent but he'd learnt long ago that there were very few women he could trust. Apart from a handful, all had let him down in the past. Besides, he had no time for a woman in his life. He opened his eyes and looked at the closed door. 'Two weeks and five months,' he muttered, before brushing all thoughts of her aside and continuing with his work. He'd been in the middle of trying to figure out what to do with Dirk Robertson, the orthopaedic registrar. If that man caused either him or his staff any more grief, Tom was going to request that disciplinary action be taken.

Jess waved goodbye to Robbie and his mother as the seven year old was wheeled to the ward.

'Promise you'll come and see me in the morning,' he called.

'I promise,' she called back, smiling brightly. 'Gorgeous child,' she murmured, and turned to finish writing up his notes. There had been no sign of a skull fracture so, apart from keeping him in overnight for observation, Robbie was fine.

Just before six that evening, she went up to CCU to see how Ingrid was doing. The ward sister informed her that the surgery had gone well and both Nicola and Dirk predicted a full recovery for the young girl.

The child's grandmother was gathering up her handbag and coat when Jess walked over to Ingrid's bedside. 'Now that the little one is sleeping, I'll go and see my son and daughter-in-law.'

'Of course.' Jess smiled. 'I've just read her notes and from the analgesics she's been given she'll, no doubt, sleep for quite a while now.'

'That's what the sister said. Well, goodnight.'

'Do you need a taxi?' Jess asked.

'The sister has organised transport for me, thank you.' Mrs Johansen's smile was weary as she walked out of the ward. Jess stood by Ingrid's beside, looking down at the small girl. If only things were easy. If only all the hurts could be made better with a kiss.

Jess sighed and shook her head slightly. Ingrid's blonde hair was splayed out on the crisp whiteness of the hospital pillows, making her look even more pale than she was. Blonde hair always reminded Jess of her sister Linda and right now, she didn't want to think about her sibling. She frowned and turned away—right into Dirk Robertson.

She gasped in surprise, wondering how long he'd been standing behind her. Both of his hands grasped her arms and Jess quickly took a step back, shifting out of his reach.

'Didn't mean to startle you,' he replied, smiling brightly. 'What a surprise to find you here.'

He didn't sound too surprised. Jess went to sidestep him but he blocked her path. She tried the other way and he followed her.

'We're almost dancing,' he said in an intimate whisper. 'So what do you say, Jess? When shall we have our date?'

Jess clenched her jaw and counted to ten. She didn't have much patience left to deal with Dirk. 'Is it possible to discuss this somewhere other than around the patients?'

He raised his eyebrows as though she were propositioning him and she felt sick. 'Sure, sweetie.'

'Ugh,' she groaned, and tried to sidestep him again. This time he didn't object and followed her back to the nurses' station.

'Where do you want to go?' he whispered close to her ear, and Jess couldn't control the involuntary shiver of disgust that crept down her spine.

'Here is fine,' she said, stopping in the hallway just outside CCU. 'Dirk, I'd just like to say that I will *never* go out with you. We aren't compatible and, although I've said this before, I'll say it again. I'd appreciate it if you didn't ask me out. Ever again!'

'Why?' he asked, not at all chastised by her words.

Jess hung onto her temper—but only just. 'Because you're not my type.'

'Then who is your type?' Dirk asked.

'I am,' a deep voice said from behind her, and she swivelled around to see Tom leaning against the wall. 'And she's my type.'

Dirk laughed. 'You've got to be joking. You haven't dated anyone for years.'

'How would you know?' Tom countered.

'Nah. You're just trying to protect her. You only met her today.'

'It was an instant attraction.' Tom came closer. 'I'd watch my step if I were you, Robertson. You're already on thin ice.'

Jess watched in alarm as the two men eyeballed each other for a long second before Dirk turned on his heel and strode back into CCU.

'Sorry about that,' Tom said with a crooked smile. Jess shook her head and glared at him. 'He shouldn't bother you again.'

'Oh, you were apologising for *him*? I thought you were apologising for *your* behaviour.'

He looked amazed. 'What have I done wr—'

'Only destroyed my reputation.'

'Destroyed it? I thought I'd saved it.'

'What a hero,' Jess said blandly.

Tom frowned and then glanced around at their present

location. He opened a door to a small cleaning room and motioned for her to go inside.

'I'm not going in there,' she stated.

'Well, it's better than having this discussion in the middle of the corridor.'

'What discussion? All you need to do is apologise for your high-handedness and we'll leave it at that.' She watched as Tom's jaw clenched and a hint of annoyance flashed in his eyes.

'In.' He pointed to the room, his body rigid, brooking no argument. Jess sighed and headed into the room.

'Satisfied?'

Tom flicked on the light and closed the door. 'First of all, I wasn't being high-handed.'

'Well, you are now.'

That stopped him for a moment but he continued. 'Perhaps, but it's called for. Since I got back this morning, I've read several complaints from other female staff members about Dirk asking them out and not taking no for an answer.'

'So what do you plan to do, Tom? Date the entire female staff of A and E?'

'Now, now, Jessica,' he said, his brisk tone disappearing. 'Sarcasm doesn't become you. I've already spoken to Jack Holden about Dirk—uh, Jack's the professor of surgery here. His wife, Kathryn, is the director of orthopaedics— and together we're trying to resolve the problem. In the meantime, I don't need my senior registrar constantly being annoyed by a junior orthopaedic registrar who's too stupid to take no for an answer.'

'Don't you realise what type of gossip your comment, not to mention your attitude, will stir up?'

He waved her concern away. 'It's just another story to be added to the list.'

'Oh, that's right, I forgot. You're positive that all hospital gossip pertains to you.'

Tom's smile increased as he gazed into her eyes. Jess started to feel a little uncomfortable in the intimate little closet. 'It won't only pertain to just me—now.'

'Which is my point exactly. Two weeks and five months,' Jess told him. 'With my name forever being linked with yours.'

'It could be worse,' he told her.

Jess scowled at him. 'I suppose you're going to suggest we go out for dinner to discuss things further.'

'No.' His gaze held hers and Jess found herself on unstable ground. The blue depths of his eyes contained a hint of regret before it quickly disappeared, to be replaced by one of aloofness. It intrigued her and she didn't want to be intrigued by Thomas Bryant. 'I have plans.'

Why did she feel a sudden pang of disappointment? Perhaps it was just as well, she rationalised as she stared into his eyes. The vision of sitting across a candlelit table from Tom appealed to her far too much. He was a dangerous man. In less than twenty-four hours she was having all sorts of intimate thoughts about him. It wouldn't do!

Tom watched as she became momentarily lost in her own thoughts. The eyes were the windows to the soul and right now he was getting the briefest glimpse of Jessica's. She was attracted to him and she wasn't at all happy about it. The knowledge made him feel empowered.

Jess realised he was waiting for her to say something and she racked her brain for a witticism, but all she could focus on was how small this closet was. She forced her previous annoyance with him to return and, after raising her chin slightly, said, 'Well, I guess there's nothing else to say except that I'm secretly hoping Dirk won't say anything to anyone else about what you implied.'

Tom shook his head in disbelief. 'I don't think there's any chance of that. Besides, all I said was that I was your type and you were my type. I didn't say we were dating or involved or anything else. What's so wrong with that?'

Jess suddenly had a burning desire to know whether or not he was serious about that or whether he'd just said it to help her out. 'So, am I your type?'

'As a matter of fact—'

'Stop!' Jess held up her hands, accidentally brushing her fingers across his chest. She felt a zap of awareness course through her before it travelled up from her fingers, through her arm and burst throughout her body. 'I...I don't think I want to know.' Her tone was husky and she grew cross with herself for allowing him to affect her.

He leaned forward slightly, closing what little distance there was between them. 'Why not, Jessica?'

As he spoke, his breath fanned her face. Being the height she was, if she edged up on her toes slightly, her mouth would be within kissing distance. Kissing! What was she thinking?

She drew back sharply, hitting her head on a shelf.

'Are you OK?' His concern was genuine, even though there was a small smile on his face.

'I'm fine. Look, Tom. I need to go. Thanks for doing what you did, even though I think it unnecessary. Now, would you mind opening the door so we can get out of here?'

'Certainly,' he replied, and did just that. He stepped into the corridor, holding the door for Jess just as Dirk came out of CCU. Jess groaned inwardly, knowing there was now no chance of there not being any gossip about them. 'Thank you for that impromptu...meeting,' Tom said, leaving Dirk's jaw hanging open.

Jess laughed with incredulity at the way her life had been turned upside down in such a short space of time. She glanced at Tom before turning and walking away, leaving the two men to say what they would to each other. There were some things she was better off knowing nothing about.

That was the last time Jess was alone with Tom for the

next three days and even then, on Thursday, just as she was getting ready to leave, he came up and handed her a large, square filing box.

'You'll need this for tomorrow morning,' he told her, and she looked at the box in her hands. It had the letters 'C.P.' written on the lid.

'What's C.P.?'

His gorgeous mouth curved into a smile and she couldn't believe the way her pulse rate immediately increased. He was handsome and he knew it. She'd purposely kept her distance from him, hoping to dispel any rumours that were currently buzzing around about the two of them...and also in the hope of controlling her unwanted reaction to him.

She hadn't actually heard any but she knew gossip was circulating like wildfire. Many of the A and E nurses had given her little knowing smiles, and whenever both she and Tom had been in the same room she could feel people watching them. Jess was annoyed that this didn't seem to bother Tom so she was determined to be equally as non-chalant about it.

'What's C.P.?' he repeated her question with a small laugh. 'You mean no one's told you?' Jess shook her head. 'How did you manage to escape finding out about C.P. during the two weeks I was away?' Tom's smile now reached his eyes. Clearly he was enjoying her ignorance.

'I'm presuming it's some sort of meeting that's held on Friday mornings?' She waited for Tom's nod. 'I've been finishing off my research project for the last two Fridays, as I will be tomorrow morning.'

'No, you won't,' he countered.

'Yes, I will. The project deadline is next Monday and it was agreed in my employment contract that the first three Friday mornings of my roster here would be devoted to finishing my research project.'

'You're not getting out of it that easily, Jessica. When-ever I'm rostered on for C.P., so are you.'

'I'm sorry, Tom but I can't make it.'

He thought for a moment and Jess's hands itched to open up the box to see what was inside. What was C.P. and why was it such a big deal that she attend? 'I'll tell you what,' he finally said. 'If you come to this…meeting tomorrow morning, you can have the rest of the day off.'

'What? You can't do that!'

'Yes, I can. I'm the director. I can change the schedule if I see fit.'

'Who'll cover for me?'

'I will.'

Jess eyed him suspiciously. 'This C.P. meeting must mean a lot to you.'

'It does,' he replied. 'So? Do we have a deal?'

Every instinct in her body was telling her to find out exactly what C.P. was before she committed herself, but it obviously didn't matter what she thought. Tom had decided she was going to be there and that was all there was to it. Besides, it would mean that after this meeting she'd be able to concentrate on her research project until late Sunday night. From Friday afternoon until Sunday night—straight. It would be worth it.

'All right,' she finally said. 'I'll be at this meeting tomorrow morning.'

'Good.'

'Is there any material I need to read up on?'

'No.' Tom's smile had disappeared but the twinkle still remained in his eyes. Jess didn't trust him. 'All the information you'll need is right there in that box.'

'All right. I'll check it out when I get home.'

'Thank you.' He took a few steps away, his smile returning. 'See you tomorrow…Jessica.'

By the time Jess arrived home, she was extremely cross with herself. Throughout the short drive from the hospital to her apartment, all she could think about was Tom Bryant and his gorgeous eyes. As hard as she'd tried during this past week *not* to think about him, she'd invariably found her thoughts turning in that direction.

He was an attractive man, she admitted. Many of the women in the hospital were attracted to him but kept their distance. Jess quickly carried the box and her briefcase from the car to the foyer, trying to avoid the cold winds and rain.

From what she'd experienced this week, Tom had been quite…nice. Certainly he'd been a bit brisk that first morning but after the meeting they'd had in his office he'd been most…amicable. Maybe Tom hadn't been joking when he'd told Dirk that she was his type.

Jess could feel the beginnings of a headache coming on. 'Enough,' she said out loud as she switched on some music, hoping it would calm her distracted thoughts. After making herself something for dinner, she sat down on the carpet of her sparsely furnished apartment and opened the box Tom had given her.

'What?' Her jaw dropped open as she stared at its contents. A bright red rubber nose, an orange curly wig and a bright and baggy tunic were the first things she pulled out. Oversized shoes and a make-up kit followed. Below that was a folder with a list of instructions for 'Clown Patrol'.

'Tom has *got* to be kidding.' Jess shook her head as she surveyed the contents again. 'Clown Patrol?' She remembered the smile on his face and knew instantly that this was no joke. She picked up the folder and began reading her instructions, which were directions for applying the make-up in several designs and handy hints to keep your shoes and nose in place, as well as how to make animal balloons.

The first page, however, contained the mission statement for all members of the Clown Patrol. 'To bring a smile to every child's face and, for a short while, help them forget where they are and why.' It was admirable. Jess had heard of clown patrols at other hospitals but had never seen or been involved in one.

'First time for everything,' she reasoned as she picked up the baggy tunic. After changing into shorts and T-shirt, Jess pulled the tunic on. 'Cute,' she told her reflection. The make-up was next and, after settling on one of the suggested designs, she diligently applied it in front of her bathroom mirror. Pinning her hair back and tugging the wig on brought a smile to her own face. The red nose completed the outfit—except for the shoes. Returning to the living room, she read the instructions for putting the clown shoes on and practised walking around in them—only falling over twice.

When someone knocked on her door, she froze. There was no way she was answering the door dressed like a clown. Dressing up for the children was fine with her and she had no problem with her forced participation, but answering the door to a complete stranger—she didn't think so!

The knock sounded again and Jess held her breath, willing the person to go away.

'Jessica?'

'Tom?' The word rushed out in shock. What was he doing here?

'Jessica? Are you home?'

If she didn't answer the door soon, curious neighbours would start coming out into the hallway, and that was the last thing she wanted.

'Shh,' she called loudly as she hurried as best she could, given that she was still practising walking in the clown shoes, to the door. 'Keep your voice down,' she ordered. After she'd opened the door, she literally tugged him inside, resisting the urge to slam the door.

Tom grinned at her. 'Sorry. I appear to have come to the wrong apartment. I was looking for Jessica Yeoman—not Grumpy the Clown.'

'Very funny. What do you want?'

He held out a plastic bag to her. 'I forgot to include the

balloon pump. There's no way you can blow up those skinny modelling balloons without a pump.'

'Well, how nice of you to bring it over. See you tomorrow, Tom.' Jess turned to open the door, got caught up in her oversized shoes and started to fall. Within an instant, she felt Tom's warm arms clamp around her, keeping her steady.

'Whoa, there.' He laughed. 'They take a bit of getting used to.'

Jess tried to quickly untangle her feet as the scent of his aftershave overwhelmed her senses. He smelled…delicious. He felt nice and warm, too and for a split second Jess allowed herself to enjoy being held so close to Tom. The more she tried to untangle her feet, however, the worse mess she found herself in.

'Just stop moving, Jessica.' He laughed again. 'You're overbalancing *me* now.' He took a step back, but with practically all of Jess's body weight leaning against him it was too much. Over they went with Jess sprawled across Tom, their arms and legs intertwined.

Jess was appalled at her behaviour, unable to believe what had just transpired. Tom was her boss! What must he think of her? She held her breath again, trying to gauge his reaction.

She felt his chest move up and down beneath her arm and realised he was laughing. 'Stop it,' she growled, not sure whether to be indignant or relieved.

Her words simply made him laugh even more. 'The…look on…your…face,' he said between chuckles, and Jess found herself smiling. He laughed again and she found it infectious.

'What about *your* face?' she said as she managed to untangle her legs, one of the shoes coming off in the process. Tom simply continued to laugh as they both gradually sat up. They looked at each other, the mirth slowly dying in the light of their intimate situation.

Their gazes locked and unspoken communication seemed to be taking place between them. Jess had never felt this drawn to any man before and although it was starting to worry her, it appeared there wasn't a lot she could do about it.

Tom cleared his throat and started to stand. 'I'd better get going.' His tone was deep and sexy. He cleared his throat again.

'You have plans again?' she asked, noticing how husky her own voice sounded. Jess looked down at her hands, wishing she hadn't spoken.

'Yes.'

Her mobile phone shrilled to life and she groaned.

When she didn't move, Tom asked, 'Aren't you going to answer it?'

'No.'

He frowned. 'It could be the hospital.'

'It isn't,' she replied.

'How do you know?'

'Because I can tell by the way it rings.'

'What?'

'Fine, then.' Jess shuffled, one shoe on, one shoe off, over to where her mobile was sitting in a corner by the beanbag. She checked the display screen. 'See.' She held it up for him. 'It says "Linda".' She answered the call, guessing she wasn't going to get any peace from Tom until she did. 'Hang on, Linda.' She picked up the beanbag and placed it on top of the phone.

'Why?' Tom pointed to the beanbag.

Jess shrugged. 'I don't want my sister to hear our conversation.'

'You have a sister?'

'Obviously.' When he didn't move, she forced a smile and said, 'Thanks for bringing the pump around.' She shuffled over to the door.

'Sure.' Tom followed her, glancing back at the beanbag

once more. 'I'll see you in the morning,' he said with a polite smile before she closed the door behind him.

Jess leaned against the door and sighed, not wanting to think about the 'moment' that had passed between Tom and herself. She wasn't even sure how it had happened. She turned and looked through the door peep-hole, out into the hallway. Tom was standing, waiting for the lift to come up, raking a hand through his hair. 'He's dangerous,' she whispered.

What had just happened? Tom questioned himself silently. What had compelled him to take the balloon pump to Jessica in the first place? He should have followed his instinct and sent it via courier. Instead, he'd convinced himself it was on its way and it wouldn't be any imposition.

The lift doors opened and he stepped inside, unable to risk one last glance at her closed apartment door. Why didn't she have any furniture? A card table and a beanbag. That was all he'd seen, apart from the C.P. box in the middle of the floor—and why didn't she want her sister to overhear their conversation? It wasn't as though they'd been saying anything confidential.

He wondered whether Jessica had any more siblings. Families had intrigued him a lot in the past but at least now he'd made peace with the fact that he was all alone in the world. It often irritated him, the way families would squabble and fight. Didn't they know how lucky they were?

Still, it made Jessica more intriguing. Tom had read her academic transcript and, although it was excellent, he'd noticed she'd moved around a lot. Usually the registrar training rotations were for a six-month block, like the one she was doing now, but three monthly rotations could be requested and she'd done quite a few of those.

Perhaps with all her moving about, she preferred not to acquire furniture. Perhaps the other places she'd stayed at had been furnished. Why was he so curious about it?

Jessica's living arrangements were nothing to him. She had five months and one week left of her registrar training and then she'd be a qualified paediatrician. Chances were she'd be moving on to another hospital so he'd do well to keep his objectivity and stop thinking about her.

Tom walked to his old station wagon and climbed in. No other woman had made such a positive impression on him in such a short time. Usually he kept women at a distance but with Jessica…there was something about her and he couldn't put his finger on it.

Maybe it was the way she reminded him a little bit of Merle. Darling Merle. If only she were still alive, he could go and talk to her about Jessica. Merle would have known what to do. She'd have known just the right thing to say to him—but Merle was dead.

The woman had been his last foster-mother and, along with her husband Alwyn, they'd pulled Tom out of the gutter and helped him get his life back on track. They'd taught him to trust, to know that there really were people in this world who were genuinely willing to help others.

He pulled up at a stop light and waited. A vision of Merle appeared in his mind as he recalled the last time he'd seen her. He'd been holding her frail hand in his, the cardiac monitor beside her bed beeping a steady rhythm.

She'd opened her eyes and motioned for him to take the oxygen mask off her mouth and nose. Gasping, she'd told him not to shut out every person he met. 'Some will guide you and others will enrich your life. Promise me, Tommy?'

She'd waited for his affirmative reply and then she'd smiled, telling him it was time for her to be reunited with Alwyn again. Tom missed them both so very much—the only two people who had ever really cared about him.

The light turned green and he continued on his way. He'd listened and learned a lot from Alwyn and Merle during the eighteen months he'd been with them, and he tried hard to keep his promise—not to push away people who started getting too close.

That was why he preferred the company of children. They were open and forthcoming about how they felt and what they wanted. Maybe that was one of the reasons why he was drawn to Jessica. She seemed to be like him. She spoke her mind and appeared to be honest.

'Time will tell,' he murmured as he parked his car and cut the engine. Tom sat there for a moment, looking unseeingly out into the dark, wet night. Whether or not he could ever trust her was another matter, but of one thing he was certain—he was attracted to her. The way her hand had felt in his on Monday had surprised him, and tonight had confirmed it as they'd sat staring at each other. He'd seen the brief flash of desire in her green eyes and had felt its effects immediately. Jessica Yeoman was a beautiful woman—even when she was dressed up like a clown.

Tom growled and shook his head. Gathering his medical bag and coat, he climbed from the car and hurried into the large, brightly lit building.

'You're late tonight.' Clarissa greeted him.

'Sorry.'

'Everything all right?'

'Fine,' he assured her. 'How's everything been going here?'

'Arnold and Maddy are starting to show flu symptoms. Gerry's chickenpox rash has finally shown itself and no one's heard or seen Harley.'

'Gone again?' Tom frowned, wondering where the fifteen-year-old boy could be.

Clarissa nodded. 'If he has one more brush with the law they'll put him away.'

'Over my dead body!' Tom responded vehemently.

'Well, *you* would know, Doc,' Clarissa replied. 'Let's get to work.'

Tom checked out the two children showing flu symptoms

and prescribed paracetamol and a decongestant. Poor Gerry's chickenpox rash was red and sore even when covered with calamine lotion.

'Wait a minute,' he told the young boy, before rushing to the infirmary, which doubled as his office, where he found a tube of cream that had an analgesic as well as antiseptic effect. When he returned, he held the tube out to Clarissa but spoke to Gerry. 'This cream might make you feel a little better. Take away the urge to itch as well.'

Gerry only grumbled but allowed Clarissa to apply the cream. Tom checked who Gerry had been in contact with before rearranging the beds in the long room, hoping to isolate the infection as best they could. When all the children were tucked up in bed and the lights had been switched off, Tom headed wearily back to the infirmary.

He loved his work at the children's shelter as it gave him the opportunity to use his medical skills for a good cause. Many of these kids were on the streets by day, but at night they could find a warm meal and a comfy bed with no questions asked.

He sat back in his chair and closed his eyes for a brief moment. A vision of Jessica popped into his head and he groaned. What was it with this woman? Why couldn't he stop thinking about her?

When the phone on his desk shrilled to life, he snatched the receiver up with relief.

'Tom Bryant,' he said briskly.

'Hey, handsome.'

'Hi Nicola.'

'You sound tired.'

'I'm fine. What can I do for you?'

'Nothing much. Just checking up on my little brother.'

A smile twitched at the sides of his lips. Although they weren't really related, Nicola Muir was the closest thing he had to a sister, and as she was in the same boat as him, having also spent part of her childhood living with Merle and Alwyn, they'd unofficially adopted each other years ago. 'Gee, thanks. So how are your kids?'

'Good.'

'And that hubby of yours? Is he keeping you under control?'

'I'll have you know that Travis and I have a wonderful relationship where neither one dominates the other.'

'Throw out the bait and watch me reel you in.' Tom chuckled.

'That's better. It's good to hear you laughing,' Nicola replied, not at all offended by his remarks. 'So tell me…'

'Yes?' he said when she paused.

'What's this rumour at the hospital I hear about you and Jess Yeoman?'

'So *that's* the reason for your call.'

'Well, I was stuck in Theatre all day and didn't have the chance to question you. I called earlier but Clarissa said you were running late. I don't suppose you'd taken your charming registrar out for an early dinner?'

'No.'

'But you'd like to.'

Tom hesitated for a split second before saying, 'That's none of your business.'

'Aha! So you *do* like her. You should go for it, Tommy. She's great.'

'I hardly know the woman, Nicola. She may be smart and have a gorgeous set of legs, but that doesn't mean I'm going to date her.'

'But you want to,' Nicola stated firmly. 'I know you, Tom. I know you better than probably anyone.' Nicola's tone changed from teasing to serious. 'She seems…different, Tom. She reminds me of someone but I can't quite put my finger on it.'

Tom took a deep breath and raked his hand through his hair. 'She reminds you of Merle.'

Nicola gasped. 'That's it. She does. Well, not in looks—

far from it. Merle was half Jess's height and a lot older.' Tom heard the warmth radiate through Nicola's tone as she spoke fondly of the woman who'd been a foster-mother to them both. 'It's the way she expresses herself.'

Tom nodded in agreement. 'The way she says certain words. Her logical thought process. All similar.'

'Don't push her away, Tom.'

'Who said—?'

'Remember who you're talking to, Thomas Andrew Bryant. I know your track record with women. You only ever let them get so far and then you end the relationship. How is any woman supposed to fall in love with you if you don't show her the *real* you?'

'Point taken,' he said, hoping to end the discussion of his love life, non existent though it was.

'If you ever want to talk, you know where to find me,' Nicola offered, thankfully taking the hint. 'So, what's new at the shelter tonight?'

'Chickenpox,' Tom replied, grateful to be on a more neutral topic. Nicola did a very fine job in her role as surrogate sister but tonight was one night when he hadn't really wanted it.

The following morning, in the female changing rooms, Jess struggled to pin her wig in place, determined that it wouldn't fall off.

'Here, let me help you with that,' Nicola offered. They were both rostered on for Clown Patrol and Jess was actually starting to feel a bit nervous.

'I take it you've done this before?' Jess asked the urology registrar.

'Yes. It's a real blast. You'll love it.'

'What…what should I expect?'

Nicola smiled as she tugged on a curly green wig. 'Expect to have fun. Let yourself go, Jess. Think of the children and how much happiness you're going to bring them.'

Nicola turned to look at her. 'Once you see the first child's face light up, you'll feel…incredible. That I promise you.'

'OK, then. I've got a pocket full of balloons and my…pump? Oh, no. Where's my pump?' She'd practised for hours the previous night, determined to master the art of those squeaky modelling balloons. Her first few attempts had looked nothing like the picture, but eventually she'd been quite proud of her giraffe and had placed him by her futon bed—a position of honour.

'You're doing the balloons?'

'Yes.'

'Wow. You're game.'

'What do you mean?'

Nicola shrugged as she located Jess's pump on the floor beneath a chair. 'Just that when Tom's rostered on, he usually does the balloons. Normally, it's the senior member of staff who does them.'

'That rat fink,' Jess mumbled but clear enough for Nicola to hear. 'I was up all night, practising doing those little animals *and* walking in these silly shoes.' Jess shook her head. 'He even had the nerve to drop the pump off.'

'Tom?'

'Yes.'

'He came around to your home?'

'Yes.' Jess was still scowling.

'Tom came to your home?' Nicola asked again, obviously in shock. 'Tom—who never gets involved with any member of staff? I guess the rumours are really true, then.'

'Huh? Oh, them.' Jess smiled. 'Don't believe everything you hear, Nicola. Right.' She consulted the clock on the wall. 'We'd better get going. We wouldn't want the great Thomas Bryant to come looking for us,' Jess remarked as she hurried towards the door.

CHAPTER THREE

JESS *loved* clown patrol. Nicola had been right. The first smile Jess had brought to one of the children's faces touched her heart for ever. She blew up a balloon and twisted it expertly into an animal before presenting it to a happy four-year-old.

'Impressive,' Tom said close to her ear, and Jess felt extremely proud of her accomplishments. If the other three members besides Nicola wondered at her doing the balloon animals, they didn't say a word. The six of them went, some running, some on scooters, up and down each ward, honking their horns and ringing bells. They told jokes, did cartwheels and magic tricks.

Tom was amazing. He really let himself go and Jess wondered how any member of staff could think him arrogant. Just seeing him with the children, the way he charmed them all, was amazing. He was brilliant with them and she realised there was a lot he could teach her during her time here.

Afterwards, they gathered in the doctors' tearoom for a well-earned rest. It had been three hours in total that they'd been out 'on patrol', but to Jess it had been over in the blink of an eye.

'Nice of you to join us today, Tom,' Nicola remarked in surprise as she crossed to the urn. 'Coffee?'

'Yes, thanks.' Tom sat back in the chair, still wearing his clown gear. 'That was a great clown patrol,' he said. Everyone but Jess stared at him as she was too busy trying to get out the thousand-and-one hairclips that had kept her wig in place. Tom smiled at her attempts, resisting the urge to help her. 'Did you enjoy it, Jessica?' he asked.

'It was…fantastic.' Jess smiled at him, her green eyes dancing with merriment. Tom returned her smile, feeling happy with the outcome. She'd performed admirably, and as she'd had only one night to practise her balloon-modelling he'd been incredibly proud of her accomplishment.

'Although,' Jess continued, 'I think I'll need to practise my poodle. One of them came out looking more like a German shepherd with the mumps!'

They all laughed and any tension the other staff might have felt at Tom's presence vanished. They continued to talk over more of the memorable moments of the patrol. 'When do we do the next one?' Jess directed her query to Tom.

'Our team is rostered on next month so you'll have time to practise your poodle.'

'I intend to,' she replied, quite seriously. She'd had a ball, especially as it had given her a glimpse of the *real* Tom Bryant. The only problem now was that Jess had liked what she'd seen.

Once they'd all recovered, Jess and Nicola returned to the changing rooms. They were in the middle of removing their make-up, still discussing their morning, when Nicola stopped what she was doing and glared at Jess. 'Are you *sure* the rumours about you and Tom aren't true?'

Jess laughed. 'Positive. I've only worked with him for a week. I hardly know him.'

'Really?' Nicola responded, but she sounded as though she still didn't believe her.

'Why would you think otherwise?'

'Well, Tom's never joined us for coffee afterwards before.'

'Oh. Well, then, how did you know how he took his coffee? He didn't tell you, yet you handed him black coffee with sugar. Are you sure you're not interested in him yourself?'

Nicola choked on a laugh. 'No. No. I'm a happily married woman with two children. No…Tom isn't my type. Besides, *you* were definitely taking everything in. Watching me make him coffee.'

Jess squirmed a little but was glad to hear Nicola say she wasn't interested in Tom. 'Well…I…um…was interested in how he took his coffee. I like knowing little details about people.'

'I see. So the next time Tom just happens to drop by your home, you'll know how he takes his coffee.'

'Something like that.' Jess turned away and continued to change. She took the C.P. box, back to Tom's office and was surprised at her disappointment when his secretary told her that he wasn't around. Jess pulled herself together, told his secretary she wouldn't be in until Monday morning and took her leave of the hospital. Her research project was her first priority as her Monday deadline was her second extension and there wouldn't be a third. She'd already lost the time she'd planned to spend on it last night but the diversion of balloon-modelling had been well worth it.

Eight hours later, she rose from the floor and stretched her tired and aching muscles. She really ought to think about getting some furniture if she was going to be here for the next six months. Then again, she'd only signed the lease for six weeks.

'You're terrified of putting down roots,' she said out loud as she walked into the kitchen. 'No, that's not it. Face facts. Ever since Scotty died, you've never found anywhere you could call home,' she mumbled.

Life had been different when her brother Scott had been alive. Their father, a local politician who'd worked hard at his career to move up the party ladder, was the most two-faced person she'd ever met.

Whilst Scott had been alive, their father had actively campaigned for disability rights, and people had believed him, all because his son had been disabled. It had won him popularity and public acclaim. At home it had been a different story—he'd mostly ignored Scott completely.

He had the same attitude towards her. He was publicly proud that his daughter had become a doctor, yet when they were alone he ridiculed her for stepping out on her own. Why couldn't she be like Linda? Why couldn't she do as she was told? Politicians' daughters didn't become doctors! There was no need for her to work. He'd take care of her. She had a position in society that he expected her to fill.

Her mother never said a word and supported her husband in every way possible. As did her younger sister, Linda. Linda—the gorgeous daughter. Linda—the child her parents had favoured since her birth. Linda—the sister who had demanded everything her own way for as long as Jess could remember.

'Sour grapes?' Jess shook her head. She was twenty-nine years old, and as she'd matured she'd become more tolerant of Linda's attitude. More tolerant of the phone calls that stretched on for hours. More tolerant of the way Linda didn't seem to care at all about Jess's work.

Her stomach growled, breaking her reverie. She hadn't eaten since lunch, which had been a quick sandwich grabbed from a vending machine on her way out of the hospital. She opened the fridge door and, after turning her nose up at the four-day-old Chinese leftovers, grabbed her coat and keys and headed out to a restaurant. She should have ordered in and kept on working but she was feeling restless. Getting out would help clear away the cobwebs.

She drove to an Italian restaurant near Chinatown and enjoyed a lovely meal of spaghetti marinara. Being a Friday night, the city was alive with fun and frivolity and Jess was glad she'd come.

She'd grown used to the stares she received as a woman dining alone, and when people tried to join her, either in a group or men trying to pick her up, she'd firmly and politely refuse.

After paying the waitress, she browsed through Chinatown and was delighted to find a balloon-modelling kit. She purchased it at once and walked back to her car with a smile on her face.

The rain had definitely settled in and she checked the road carefully before pulling out into the traffic. The shops were closing and everyone was starting to head home. Quite a few more cars were on the road than when she'd arrived. Not being familiar with the streets and traffic flow, Jess was forced to drive a few blocks south before she could head back north again. She stopped at a red light and reached over to take another look at the balloon kit. The next time she was on Clown Patrol, she'd be making perfect poodles—impressing Tom in the process.

The light turned green and Jess slowly accelerated, the Jaguar XJ6 purring nicely as she drove. The end of that road led onto Whitmore Square and Jess watched the on-coming headlights, waiting for a moment to pull out. With the rain now bucketing down, she made sure she took her time. The last thing she needed right now was to have an accident.

Finally, the road was clear and she accelerated around the corner, heading northwards again. A movement in her peripheral vision made her glance to her right and in an instant she realised that a car was trying to overtake her. 'Fool,' she muttered, and slowed her car.

Before she knew what was happening, there was a screech of brakes followed by a loud thud, and then she saw a body come flying off the bonnet of the car beside her. The car skidded again before taking off. Jess braked hard to avoid the person who'd been hit. The figure staggered in front of her car before falling into a heap in the gutter. Jess swerved to the side of the road and stopped the car. She flicked on her hazard lights with a shaking hand and undid her seat belt, hoping the person who'd been hit was all right.

The doctor inside her came to life immediately and she rushed to the victim's side. 'Can you hear me?' It was then she realised it wasn't a man, as she'd previously thought but a boy. A boy of about fourteen or fifteen. She checked his pulse and breathed a sigh of relief when she found one.

'Can you hear me?' she called again, her hair now plastered to her face, thanks to the soaking rain. The boy murmured and her relief grew. He was regaining consciousness. 'I'm a doctor. Stay still while I check you out.' Jess reached out and touched his shoulder. 'It's all right,' she said, trying to reassure him. Instead, he lifted his head and gazed at her with wide, wild eyes.

'Don't touch me.' His tone was filled with anguish and distress, his voice breaking on the last word. He backed away from her and she reached out again.

'Wait. Stop. You may have seriously hurt yourself.'

'Leave me alone!' He scrambled to his feet, crying out in pain as he tried to move his arm. He cradled it with his good one.

'*Please*,' Jess implored, feeling more and more desperate as the moments dragged on. 'Let me help you. I'm a doctor.'

'No. Stay away,' he said as he backed away up onto the kerb. Then he turned and ran.

Jess couldn't believe it. She quickly returned to her car and grabbed her coat and medical bag while trying to still the shaking of her cold hands. She switched off her hazard lights and locked her car before heading after the boy. He couldn't have gone too far and she was now desperate to find him. He could have sustained a serious head injury. Never could she live with herself if she didn't at least try to search for him.

The streets were dimly lit and lined with trees but Jess wasn't to be discouraged. She checked a few backstreets but came up empty. She must have been searching for a good fifteen minutes when the shaking started to get worse.

She was cold and wet, and if she wasn't careful she'd be in bed with a raging fever within twenty-four hours. The heavy rain hadn't eased up for one second and Jess started to feel dejected.

Whoever the youth was, he knew these streets better than she did, and even though he was injured she couldn't find him anywhere. Then again, he hadn't wanted her help, which meant he wouldn't want to be found.

As she started heading back to her car, she saw a bright shining light at the end of one side street and instinctively turned towards it. The sign across the front of the building said it was a refuge and she thought it was worthwhile checking it out and at least leaving her details should the boy turn up for help.

She pushed open the heavy glass door with effort. Her body felt frozen and her teeth were chattering uncontrollably.

'Can I help?' a large, dark-skinned woman asked.

Jess tried to focus on her name-tag but her eyes refused to work. 'Boy,' Jess said through purple lips.

'You're looking mighty cold and wet, miss,' the woman said kindly. 'Come over here and stand by the heater.'

Jess could have hugged her. She left her medical bag on a table and held her hands out to the heater, rubbing them together to get the blood circulating again. After a few minutes, the woman brought her a hot mug of sickly sweet tea. It tasted like manna from heaven to Jess and she was extremely grateful.

'A boy,' Jess said at last, her jaw still shaking a bit. 'About fourteen or fifteen. He was hit by a car. I tried to help him but he ran off.'

'So that's why you're here,' a deep voice said from behind her, and Jess whirled around in shock, her eyes as wide and wild as the boy's had been.

'T-T-Tom?' she stuttered, gazing at him in disbelief. A wave of nausea started to rise up and she felt hot and cold flushes all over. She closed her eyes, dimly aware of her hands letting go of the mug and the muted sound it made as it crashed to the floor.

'She's going to go,' she heard Tom say, and as her knees started to give way Jess felt his firm arms about her waist. 'Jessica? Jessica?' His voice was too far off and she thankfully gave in to the blackness that engulfed her.

'You big bully,' Clarissa chastised him as she bent to pick up some of the broken mug pieces. 'Why did you have to go and scare her like that? Can't you see she's been through enough?' She stood again and sighed heavily. 'Bring her through here.'

Tom lifted Jessica into his arms, amazed at how heavy she felt. She was extremely wet, her thick woollen coat adding to the weight. He felt his own clothes begin to soak as he followed Clarissa up the corridor towards the staff quarters.

'How's Harley doing?' she asked him.

'He's fractured his left scapula and humerus and has a mild concussion.'

'In English, Tommy,' Clarissa said with a scowl. 'I don't know how often I've told you that I don't understand all that medical mumbo jumbo and yet you still spout it at me.'

'Sorry,' he said with a smile. 'He's broken his shoulder and upper arm. He'll have headaches for about the next two weeks and will probably be nauseated.'

'Thank you,' Clarissa said, and held open the door for Tom. 'Let's get her out of those wet clothes before she catches pneumonia.'

'Uh...perhaps you'd better...' He stopped and realised he was behaving like an adolescent schoolboy. He was a doctor, for heaven's sake. Just because he was attracted to Jessica, it didn't mean he couldn't help her out—stop her from getting pneumonia. Besides, Clarissa was in the room. 'Never mind,' he grumbled, and Clarissa gave a hearty chuckle.

'Well, ain't that a first?' she laughed but stopped immediately when Tom glared at her. Together they managed to take off Jessica's saturated clothing and get her beneath the covers.

'Oh, cute underwear,' Clarissa murmured with a smile, and then chuckled softly as Tom grunted a noncommittal reply and turned away.

'I'll stay with her,' she volunteered. 'You go see what's happening with young Harley. At least we know where he is now.'

'True.'

'Oh, and can you get someone to clean up the broken mug?'

'Sure.' Tom took a few steps out of the small room before taking one last look at Jessica, lying there in the small camp bed. Her face was pale and the colour of her damp hair looked to be an even richer auburn. She was...beautiful. 'Harley,' he murmured, and turned on his heel, leaving Clarissa to attend to Jessica. He stopped by the kitchen on his way to talk to one of the kitchen-hands but found the mess had already been attended to.

He strode back to where he'd left Harley, in the capable hands of the children's shelter's live-in nurse, Betty. Betty had retired from nursing many years ago. Her husband was the caretaker here and they'd been lifelong friends with Alwyn and Merle.

'How's he doing?' he asked Betty as he walked into the infirmary.

'He's resting. I've cleaned up his head and given him something for the pain. The old X-ray machine is still warming up so as soon as it's ready I'll get you to give me a hand and we'll get him sorted out.'

'Sure.'

'Who was that I saw you carrying through the corridor?'

'A woman who saw the accident and wanted to help.'

'She came looking for him? That's different, especially

as Harley had obviously run away from her. I tell you, I got such a fright when he burst in through those doors.' Betty patted her chest. 'Anyway, it's nice that she came looking for him. Shows she cares.'

'She's a doctor.'

'One of yours?' Betty raised her eyebrows when Tom nodded.

'She's my registrar.'

Betty sighed. 'What are you going to do?'

Tom shrugged. 'Wait until she regains consciousness and see how she's feeling.'

Betty frowned. 'So you don't mind her knowing you work in this place?'

'It's no great secret. I just choose who I tell, that's all.'

'People you can trust,' Betty added with a nod. 'And do you trust this woman?'

Tom hesitated. 'Jessica? I hardly know her,' he offered.

'Well, she's all right by me. Anyone who risks looking for a sick child in this weather is a person who has their head on their shoulders. Someone who might be…trustworthy.'

'I don't know.'

'Well you work with her.'

'I've only worked with her for this last week. I was away, remember?'

'Yes, dear. Although the number of hospital staff who know about your…nocturnal activities, shall we call them, is forever increasing.'

'Yes, but they're all people I trust. People who also want to help these children.'

'I know, Tommy. I was just teasing.' Betty gave him a hug. 'I know you're a private man and that you keep yourself to yourself. You put up wall after wall to keep people out and I can understand why. Yet with the children you give and keep on giving. You're a good man, Thomas. You deserve to find a woman who might bring you a little happiness and understanding.'

'You got all that from me carrying a woman down a corridor?' Tom asked, and shook his head in amazement.

'No,' Betty replied, the teasing gone. 'It was the way your face softened when you said her name.'

Jess felt a shiver tingle its way down her body. Slowly she opened her eyes. Where was she? Mental alarm bells started to ring but she remained still, her gaze searching for something familiar in the dimly lit room.

'Ah, you're awake.' The voice came from her left and Jess slowly turned her head in that direction. 'You're at the children's shelter,' the woman told her. 'Remember? You came in looking for a boy who'd been hit?'

Yes. It was all coming back to her now. Jess remembered feeling cold—so terribly cold—and something else. She'd broken a mug. No, that wasn't it. 'Tom!' She whispered his name, her gaze wide.

'That's right,' the woman said. 'You saw Tom and then you passed out. My name, by the way, is Clarissa. I work here.'

Jess started to sit up and she realised she wore nothing but her underwear. 'My clothes!' she gasped and it was at that moment that her head started to pound. She lay back on the pillow, pulling the blankets more closely around her.

'Take it easy,' Clarissa advised. 'Your clothes were soaked. We had to take them off you,' Clarissa continued, 'or you would have caught a terrible cold.'

'We?' Jess whispered, and closed her eyes, waiting for the other woman's answer. Please, don't let her say Tom, she prayed. Please!

Clarissa ignored her question. 'As it is, I'm not sure you'll escape after-effects. The last time I felt your forehead, you were still quite hot.' Clarissa put some clothes on the bed. 'Here. Put these on and you'll feel better.'

When Jess didn't move, Clarissa said kindly, 'Do you need some help getting dressed?'

Jess wasn't sure. Even though she was feeling humiliated and embarrassed—especially at the thought of Tom Bryant undressing her—Clarissa was being helpful and nice.

'I think I might need some help. Thank you.' Jess started to sit up and raised a shaky hand to her temples. 'My head's pounding.'

'I can imagine.' Clarissa helped her to dress, remarking how the clothes weren't too bad a fit, especially as Jess was so tall. The track pants were warm and she only had to roll them up twice. The navy skivvy and jumper were, again, a bit long in the arms but it meant her fingers could stay warm.

'Thank you,' Jess replied.

'You're welcome dear. Tom said to bring you through to the infirmary when you were ready.'

'The infirmary?'

'Let's go,' Clarissa said as she opened the door. Jess followed the other woman down a corridor, realising she wasn't going to volunteer any information—especially about Tom and why he was here.

'Here we are,' she said after opening a door. 'Look who's awake,' Clarissa remarked to whoever was in the room. Feeling a bit apprehensive, Jess forced her legs to work and as she walked in she saw Tom sitting at a desk, writing notes, his hand about to pick up the phone. A woman, who Jess guessed to be in her late sixties, stood next to the examination couch, monitoring the boy.

'I'll leave you all to it,' Clarissa said, and closed the door behind her.

'How are you feeling?' Tom asked as his gaze quickly washed over her. Jess felt a stirring of excitement in the pit of her stomach but squashed it immediately.

'Warmer.'

'You don't look too bad in my clothes,' he remarked. 'Just as well you're so tall.' He smiled at her.

These were *Tom's* clothes? Jess unconsciously raised a hand to touch her top, amazed at how embarrassed she felt to be wearing Tom's clothes. She looked down at the floor, using her hair as a screen while she collected her thoughts. She cleared her throat and raised her head again. 'Um…' She motioned to the boy. 'How is he?' Jess rubbed her hands together and paced around the room a little, keeping the blood flowing.

'Fractured scapula, fractured humerus and mild concussion.' While Tom spoke, he poured a glass of water and handed her two paracetamol tablets. Jess took them without complaint. 'This is Betty,' he said as the woman handed him an X-ray. 'Radiograph of his head.' Tom held the X-ray up to the light. 'As you can see, there's no evidence of skull fractures.'

'So when is he going to the hospital?'

'He's not.'

'What? Tom, he—'

'I know, Jessica,' Tom said firmly. 'I know he needs treatment, which is exactly what I'm in the process of organising.'

'But you're not going to take him to the hospital,' she stated.

'There's no point. Things work differently in this world,' he told her. 'We still uphold the law, but if I took Harley to the hospital, Social Welfare would need to be involved— and right now that's the last thing Harley needs.'

'So what are you going to do? Operate on him yourself?'

'Of course not,' Tom growled. 'Even though I am qualified to perform surgery,' he clarified.

'But you don't have the equipment? The instruments? The plates or wires he'll no doubt need to fix his fractures?'

'No,' he said, carefully holding onto his temper. Jess could tell she was beginning to push him to the edge but

Harley's well-being was at stake and Tom was refusing to take him to the hospital.

'What's so wrong with Welfare getting involved?'

'You don't know the details,' he told her. 'And I refuse to discuss it any further,' he added when she opened her mouth to say something else. Tom picked up the phone and punched in a number. 'Jack. It's Tom. Is Kathryn available?' he asked, his tone professional. 'I have a fifteen-year-old boy here with fractured scapula and humerus. Hit and run.' Tom paused for a moment. 'Yeah. He's very lucky.' Another pause. 'Harley.' Tom glanced over at Betty and nodded. 'Right. We'll meet Kathryn at her private operating rooms. Thanks.'

Tom hung up. 'Let's get him ready to transport. Jessica, we'll probably need your help. With Kathryn coming out, Jack will need to stay home and take care of their kids. Another pair of hands may be just what we need. I'll get the car,' he said, and left her alone with Betty.

'Let's get Harley ready for transfer,' Betty suggested.

Jess shook her head, still staring at the door Tom had just left through.

'Jessica?'

She turned and looked at Betty. 'Call me Jess.'

'You prefer it?' Betty asked as she hauled out a portable stretcher.

Jess shrugged. 'It's easier. Just don't ever call me Jessie. That, I hate.'

'Noted,' Betty said as they put the stretcher together.

'Why doesn't Tom want Welfare involved?' Jess asked quietly. 'I don't understand.'

'Harley's been missing for the past few days and the police have been very interested in finding him. They want to question him about a few break-ins.'

'So if Welfare gets involved, they'll hand him over to the police?'

'Only if he's done something wrong.'

'And Tom wants to protect him?'

'If Harley has broken the law, Tom will ensure he gets the punishment he deserves. Right now, though, Harley is badly injured and in need of medical attention. By not taking him to the hospital, Tom is merely buying Harley some time. I'm sure Tom will contact his friend at the police station to find out the latest information on the break-ins they want to question Harley about.'

Betty smiled at Jess. 'Tom's protecting Harley against being put into yet another foster-home when it's the last thing the boy needs right now.' She looked around the room and nodded. 'Right, I think that's everything so let's move him.' They worked together to transfer Harley to the stretcher and then, with Betty leading the way, they carried him out to the front of the shelter.

Clarissa was waiting with a large umbrella and Tom had actually reversed a station wagon right up onto the footpath, with the back of the vehicle facing the doors. As he opened the tailgate, she saw that the back seat had been folded forward, giving more room in the back. 'Betty and Jessica, you stay in the back with him.' He turned to Clarissa. 'I'll call as soon as he's out of surgery.' With that, Tom helped manoeuvre the stretcher into the car. When everyone was ready, he climbed behind the wheel and carefully eased the car off the kerb onto the road.

The rain hadn't eased up one bit and Jess shivered in spite of herself. 'Are you all right, Jess?' Betty asked, and she nodded. The car was warm, which helped.

'It's not far,' Tom said as he navigated the traffic. Ten minutes later, he pulled the car into a driveway and came to a stop. A woman with shoulder-length auburn hair, almost the same colour as Jess's, was waiting impatiently by a door.

'Thanks, Kathryn,' Tom said as he came around to open the tailgate.

'My pleasure. Hi, Betty,' she said as they started to get

the stretcher out. 'Hi,' she said to Jess. 'I don't believe we've met.'

'Kathryn, this is Jessica Yeoman, my new registrar.'

'Call me Jess.'

'Hi, I'm Kathryn Holden. Head of Orthopaedics at the hospital.' She looked Jess over. 'So you're the registrar Dirk's been bothering,' Kathryn said with a nod. 'Hopefully, we've now rectified the matter.' She turned her attention to Harley and looked him over quickly as they carried him inside. 'Straight through to the operating theatre at the back,' she advised, but Tom led the way and knew where he was going.

'Jess, this is Frances Gray—she'll be Harley's anaesthetist for the night,' Kathryn introduced. 'Betty, have you got the X-rays?'

'I certainly do.'

Kathryn took a look at them, figuring out what sort of equipment she'd require. 'It's not as bad as I'd thought.'

Tom was talking to Frances, discussing what analgesics he'd given Harley. Jess was amazed at the whole set-up. Here was this boy—this boy Tom didn't want to take to the hospital simply to avoid the hassles of bureaucracy — being treated by the head of Orthopaedics and one of the best paediatric anaesthetists.

'Jess. How's your orthopaedics?'

'A bit rusty,' Jess admitted. 'I haven't done much since my internship.'

'You've just been drafted.'

'What about Tom?'

'I'm sure we can find something for Tom to do,' Kathryn said with a smile. 'Right. Let's get this show on the road. Consent form?'

Tom came over to her side. 'Harley is legally a ward of the State and therefore Clarissa accepts the role of guardian.' Tom took a piece of paper out of his back pocket.

'I've explained the operation to Clarissa, so here's the signed consent form.'

'Terrific. Now, let's get started.' As it turned out, both Tom and Jess assisted Kathryn and in no time she had Harley's injuries all sorted out.

'He's all yours, Frances,' Kathryn announced as they de-gowned. 'I presume you'll be watching him closely to-night?' she asked Tom.

'Yes. Betty and I will take it in shifts.'

Jess listened to what everyone else was saying but all the while she was starting to feel progressively worse. The paracetamol Tom had given her was starting to wear off and the pounding in her head was returning. She walked over to the side of the room and leaned against the wall, closing her eyes.

'Jessica?' Tom's voice was soft yet close and her eyelids opened marginally in response. He was standing in front of her, a concerned look on his face.

'I think everything's starting to take its toll.'

He reached out a hand and felt her forehead and she closed her eyes again. 'You're starting to feel hot again. I'll get you some paracetamol.'

'No,' she breathed softly. 'It's too late.'

'What?'

'Migraine.'

'I'll see what Kathryn's got.'

'Ergotamine,' she whispered as the pounding increased. This time her eyes remained closed. He returned a few minutes later with the medication she'd requested and watched as Jess swallowed the tablets.

'Thanks.'

'I think I'd better get you home. Stay here, I'll be right back.'

Moments later, Kathryn came over and took her hand. 'You poor thing. Tom told me what happened and how you were out looking for the boy. At least you're not working on the weekend and can hopefully sleep the migraine off. Come on. I'll help you to the door.'

Jess was in no position to argue. After Tom had seated her in the front of the station wagon and strapped on her belt, Jess willed the medication to start working. Although she knew he was going slowly and carefully, avoiding any bumps that might increase the pain, Jess just wanted the ride to be over. He stopped at the shelter and retrieved her keys and wet clothes before driving her home.

In the lift, heading up to her apartment, Jess could hardly stand the sensation of movement. Tom had one arm around her shoulders for support but the instant he'd unlocked her door she rushed to the bathroom and was sick.

'Jessica.' Tom's tone was full of concern and Jess was warmed by it. She felt a little better now and allowed him to scoop her up into his arms and carry her through to the bedroom. She snuggled her face into his neck, breathing in the wonderful scent of his spicy aftershave. 'A futon. I should have guessed,' he mumbled, but Jess was too exhausted to analyse anything.

He took off the jumper and track pants without any comment from her, and when she was finally lying down, her head resting on the pillow, she sighed with contentment. She felt Tom's hand stroking her hair off her face. It felt wonderful.

She tried to open her eyes but couldn't. Sleep was starting to claim her, and as she drifted off she felt Tom's lips brush lightly across her own.

Once Jessica was asleep, Tom hunted around for a bucket in case she felt the need to be sick again. Instead, all he found was an empty plastic ice-cream container. 'It'll have to do,' he muttered. He found her migraine tablets and placed two by the bed with a glass of water. He noticed the balloon giraffe on the other side of her bed and smiled. Had it been only that morning that they'd been on clown patrol?

Tom shook his head and left her alone to sleep. As he made his way back to the door, he stepped over the spread of papers and books which was obviously the research project she was working on. He wondered how far behind this migraine would put her? She'd said it was due on Monday and he hoped she'd make her deadline.

He ensured the door was locked as he let himself out then rode the lift back down to his car. He collected Harley and Betty from Kathryn's surgery and drove back to the shelter. It would be a long night, monitoring their patient, so far the boy's recovery had been uncomplicated and both Frances and Kathryn were very pleased.

'I'll take the first shift,' he told Betty after Harley was settled in the infirmary. Tom checked the boy's vital signs and noted them on the chart before sitting down at his desk. His thoughts turned immediately to Jessica. He empathised with her about the migraine and hoped she'd be over it soon. He raked a hand impatiently through his hair and closed his eyes, remembering the silkiness of her rich auburn mane, the smoothness of her skin, the softness of her lips.

He exhaled slowly. When he'd undressed her the first time, he'd been surprised to find she wasn't all skin and bones, as most tall, thin women were. Instead, she was perfectly proportioned. It had been hard to switch into doctor mode, especially when he'd undressed her the second time.

And her underwear!

'Stop it,' he growled. 'You're a doctor.' Tom stood and checked Harley's vital signs, just to prove the point to himself. He sat back down again and closed his eyes. His lips twitched marginally as he recalled the pink bunny underwear. What type of woman wore underwear with pink bunnies on them?

Jessica did.

It wasn't that he didn't *like* the bunnies, far from

it. Just that he hadn't expected them. 'Get out of my head.'
He turned his attention to the paperwork on his desk, determined to push every thought of the beautiful Jessica
Yeoman away. Moments later, the memory of his lips
brushing against hers intruded.

'What on earth possessed you to kiss her?' he whispered
fiercely. It had complicated everything—everything he'd
worked so hard for. For years he'd built walls about himself
to keep people away, yet in the space of five days several
were starting to crumble.

'If you're not careful, you'll be falling for her—and that
will *never* do!'

CHAPTER FOUR

THE next morning, Jess woke from a wonderful dream. She stretched and yawned, enjoying the warmth of the bedcovers. She lay there for a moment, trying to figure out what day it was. When she realised it was Saturday and that she wasn't rostered on, it made her feel even better.

Slowly, with one thought after another, her good mood started to vanish as she remembered what had happened yesterday and the research project that still awaited her attention. She glanced at the clock and was surprised to see that it was almost ten o'clock. She hadn't slept that late in years—then again, she hadn't had a migraine in years.

With everything that had gone on yesterday, from the clown patrol to being soaked through when looking for Harley, Jess was surprised to find she wasn't feeling too bad. No after-effects from being drenched or from her migraine, which was unusual.

Even so, she took it easy as she slowly sat up in bed and swivelled her legs around, kicking an empty plastic container. She frowned, momentarily wondering how it had materialised there. There was also a glass of water and her migraine tablets beside the bed.

'Tom,' she whispered.

Jess sat there for a few more minutes, thinking. It had been very thoughtful of him to put the container, water and tablets where she would find them. Very thoughtful indeed. In her extremely limited experience with men, no one else had ever thought of her needs before.

Then she realised she wasn't wearing her usual nightshirt, just her underwear. Her face burned with embarrassment and she closed her eyes, groaning in disbelief. He would have seen her pink bunny underwear—twice!

She felt humiliated for a moment but rationalised that there really wasn't anything she could do to change the situation and, besides, she liked her pink bunnies and the rest of the underwear in her drawer. She had a range of bright and colourful cartoon characters, as well as some cute teddy bears—and bunnies, of course.

Taking a deep breath, she walked slowly to the bathroom and started the shower. She hadn't had a migraine quite that bad for some time and usually she was out of action for a few days. Last night, though, she'd had the most wonderful dream. She'd been on holiday in the majestic Blue Mountains in New South Wales. Cut off from phone, fax and email. Her sister, the hospital—no one—had been able to contact her for a whole week, and Jess had marvelled in the peace and quiet. She finished her shower and dressed, heading for the kitchen as she recalled more of her dream.

Her only companion had been a man. He'd had dark hair and the most incredible blue eyes. His lips had brushed across hers and she'd felt herself floating amongst the clouds, enjoying the sensations he'd evoked. She closed her eyes while she waited for the kettle to boil, recalling the man of her dream.

His arms around her had been strong and supportive, making Jess feel safe. His eyes had been glazed with desire when he'd looked at her, making Jess feel sexy. His lips had promised the most passionate kiss she'd ever experienced. Jess hadn't been disappointed.

She raised a hand to her mouth and gently rubbed her fingers across it. The action brought back a memory and her eyelids snapped open. 'Tom,' she breathed, and shook her head as though to clear the thoughts.

The kettle boiled but switched itself off automatically. Jess didn't move. 'Tom.' She whispered his name again and with a shock realised that *he'd* been the man in her dream. The man who, she could have sworn, had pressed his lips to her own. Had Tom kissed her last night? She vaguely remembered him bringing her home and putting her to bed.

'Oh, no,' she groaned, and buried her face in her hands as the memory of being sick in the bathroom intruded. Tom had been wonderful but, still, no woman wanted a man to see her like that. 'Face it, Jess,' she told herself as her mobile phone rang. 'No man would be interested in a woman after witnessing a spectacle like *that*.' She picked up the phone, in no mood to hear about her sister's Friday night. 'What now, Linda?'

'See! You forgot to check the mobile phone display that time,' Tom's deep voice said on the other end of the line. Jess felt herself blush and was glad he couldn't see her. 'How are you feeling?'

'Quite good, actually.'

'You sound surprised.'

'It usually takes me a few days to get over migraines.'

'How often do they come?' he asked, his tone a bit brisk.

'Worried I'll get one on duty?'

'It did cross my mind,' he replied honestly.

'The last bad one I had was seven years ago.'

'What do you classify as bad?'

'I was bedridden for a week and constantly throwing up. My doctor almost hospitalised me.'

'That is bad. What triggered it?'

'My brother died.' Jess found it hard to keep the emotion out of her tone as she said the words. She still missed Scott, far too much.

'I see. So since then you've only had mild migraines?'

'Yes.'

'And those are the ones that keep you in bed for a few days?'

'Yes.'

'So what do you call last night's migraine?'

'More of an…extended headache. The thing was, I was able to take the medication as it was just starting. The paracetamol you'd given me earlier had helped. I had a fantastic dream,' She stopped and corrected herself. 'Uh…sleep last night and that makes all the difference in the world.' Again Jess felt her cheeks grow hot from embarrassment. She'd only had such a wonderful sleep because she'd been dreaming about him. The two of them. Together!

'OK, then. Are you ready for breakfast?'

'I don't eat breakfast. How's Harley?'

'He's progressing just fine. What do you mean, you don't eat breakfast? That's not good for you, Jessica.'

'Aren't you supposed to be at the hospital?' she countered.

'No, and stop trying to change the subject. Why don't you eat breakfast?'

'Why do you need to know?'

'Because I'm downstairs in your car with a lovely picnic breakfast. Unfortunately, as it's still raining, I need a dry place to spread the picnic rug and I noticed that you have a lot of…carpet space in your living room, so if you wouldn't mind gathering up your research papers, I'll be right up.'

'Tom. I don't think that's a goo—' Too late. He'd hung up. Jess wasn't sure what to do. She started gathering up the papers then stopped. Why was he in her car? She'd left it parked on the side of the road when she'd gone looking for Harley. She frowned and started looking around for her keys. The knock on the door shouldn't have startled her—but it did.

'Open up, Jessica. I have an assortment of goodies, all designed to tempt you.'

'Why are you doing this?' she called through the door. 'Why are you picking on me to torture?'

'Torture, eh? Well, if you think this is bad, wait until

you see what else I have up my sleeve. Now, are you going to open this door or not?'

'Not.'

'Come on, Jessica. It would be a lot easier for me if I didn't have to put everything down to use your house keys to get in.'

'So who says I want to make things easy for you?' Jess smiled to herself, enjoying their banter. She returned to the living room and gathered up the rest of her papers, making sure they all stayed in order. She heard the key go into the lock and within seconds he'd opened the door. She looked up from where she was kneeling on the floor, waiting for him to come in.

She saw a picnic basket first with a red-checked rug draped over his arm. The rest of him appeared, clad in a warm winter coat. In his other hand he held some coat-hangers covered in plastic, and Jess realised with a start that they were the clothes she'd been wearing yesterday evening. He nudged her front door closed with his foot and held out the clothes to her. 'All cleaned and ready to wear again.'

'But…there was no need.'

He shrugged as she took them from him. 'It's done. You put them away while I get this picnic organised.'

Jess took the clothes from him, murmuring her thanks. She was astonished at his thoughtfulness and again reminded herself not to listen to hospital gossip, especially where Tom was concerned.

When she returned, it was to find him laying food on the blanket that was spread out over her living-room floor. He'd removed his coat and looked incredibly sexy in black denim jeans and a navy blue jumper. Jess licked her lips but it had nothing to do with the food in front of her. 'Croissants, bagels, Danish pastries. Orange juice as well as hot coffee. What would you like to start with?'

It was then she noticed the green poodle balloon in the

centre of the rug. Jess laughed and picked it up. 'I see you found the modelling kit I bought. How do you do this? It looks so…perfect.'

'That's because it is. Don't change the subject. What would you like?'

She thought about it, feeling a little overawed. She knelt down on the opposite side to him and surveyed the food, the poodle still in her hand. 'Coffee, I think.'

'As the lady wishes,' he remarked with a smile. He poured her a cup. 'Milk? Sugar?'

'No, just black, thanks.' Jess put the balloon down, a smile still lighting her face.

Tom poured himself a cup before stretching out on the floor.

'Relaxed?' she asked, unable to believe how at home he looked in her apartment.

'Yes, as a matter of fact, I am.' He bit into a croissant. Jess sipped at her coffee and watched him. 'You're starting to bubble over with questions, Jessica,' he said after he'd swallowed his mouthful. 'Why don't you ask them?'

She nodded. 'How long have you been involved in the shelter?'

'For the last eleven years as their doctor. I've been volunteering and helping out since I was seventeen.'

'Wow! So you've been living in Adelaide all that time? You didn't get itchy feet? Want to move around?'

'No. I like it here. Of course, I did an overseas stint as part of my training but, apart from that, I've always lived in Adelaide.' He thought for a moment and then added, 'I did leave the State for a few months but that was due to dire circumstances.'

'Really? What happened?' Jess saw a momentary glint of steel in his gaze and wondered if she'd overstepped the mark.

Tom looked into his coffee-cup and then back at Jess. 'I left the State because…because of something that had hap-

pened in one of the foster families I was with.' His tone
was emotionless.

'What?' The word was out of her mouth before she could
stop it. 'Sorry,' she said immediately. 'You don't need to
answer that.'

'My past is my past. There's nothing I can do to change
it.' A vision of Renee flashed before his eyes. He could
still see her standing in front of her parents, tears streaming
down her face while she lied to them, telling them that Tom
had made unwanted sexual advances towards her. He
shrugged the image away. 'Besides,' he added, forcing a
smile, 'you've probably heard all sorts of different rumours
still circulating around the hospital.'

'See, there you go again, thinking that every rumour in
the hospital is about you. I'll have you know that I've also
been told gossip about other people in the hospital—most
of whom I don't know, but that's beside the point.'

'Which is?'

'That I try my best not to listen to what's being said.
After all, since you spoke to Dirk the other day, even *I've*
been gossiped about.'

'Oh, you were gossiped about before you arrived.' Tom
smiled naturally at her, enjoying the look of horror that
crossed her face.

'What?'

'Don't stress.' He chuckled. 'It's nothing bad. One of the
ward sisters worked with you in Canada and she reported
that you were as tall and as stunning as a model. That you
gave everything to the job and kept yourself to yourself.'

Jess gaped at him, still surprised at there being someone
at the hospital who knew her.

'But don't worry about it because I never listen to gossip,' he told her with mock solemnity.

'Really?' She didn't believe him. 'Then why was the first
thing you said to me, ''You're taller than I'd expected''?'

Tom laughed. '*Touché*! You have an excellent memory.'

He finished off his croissant and looked at her, his gaze intense, the teasing gone. 'Why do you keep yourself to yourself?' His tone was so gentle and caring that she almost crumbled.

Instead, Jess picked at a bagel, hoping that by putting a bit of food in her mouth it would give her time to compose her words. Whenever Tom laughed or smiled at her, she had a strange flurry in the pit of her stomach. It was as though butterflies lived there and whenever he turned the smile in her direction the butterflies came to life, flying around in her stomach and causing all sorts of knee-weakening, heart-pounding sensations.

She decided to turn the focus back on him. 'Why do you?'

'I asked you first.'

'I asked you second.'

He smiled, enjoying their banter. 'Because I've been let down by people too many times. I'm very careful who I trust and it takes a lot to earn it.'

'How am I doing?' she asked, knowing full well that she was on trial. She held her breath as she waited for him to answer. Whatever he said next, it would help her know in what direction he wanted to take their relationship. Right now, it was merely one of colleagues who enjoyed each other's company, but there was no denying the attraction between them.

Tom frowned thoughtfully before nodding. 'Not bad,' he murmured.

'That's quite a compliment,' she acknowledged with a smile.

'Well, I think seeing the pink bunny underwear definitely helped.' Tom kept his gaze trained on hers, watching her reaction closely. Her eyes grew wide and her cheeks flushed in embarrassment.

'Tom!'

'What?'

She spluttered for a moment. 'It's…ungentlemanly to…to bring up such a topic as a woman's underwear. Especially when you only saw it because I was unconscious.' Jess raised her hands to cover her hot cheeks.

'No. The first time you were unconscious *and* Clarissa was in the room. The second time you were…' Tom recalled just how wonderful she'd felt in his arms as he'd carried her to her bed. The way her body had melded perfectly with his own and how she'd snuggled close before he'd lowered her onto the futon.

'I was…?'

His eyes were glazed with desire as he recalled the image of her lying on the mattress before he'd carefully removed her clothes. He broke eye contact and cleared his throat. 'You were drowsy…but not unconscious.' His words had still been husky and Tom knew the attraction he felt towards Jessica increased with every minute he spent with her.

'Pure semantics,' Jess said with a flamboyant wave of her hand and toss of her head. 'You still shouldn't be discussing my underwear in this fashion.'

'I don't see that I did anything drastically wrong. I undressed you the second time to make you more comfortable. You might have become dehydrated beneath the doona with all those warm clothes on. As a doctor, I recognised this risk and, knowing how it wouldn't help your migrained state, I therefore carefully removed your clothes.'

Jess's smile disappeared. The teasing note had vanished as he'd spoken, his words becoming clipped and professional. 'Hey. I was only teasing, Tom.' Jess eyed him cautiously. 'What prompted that tone?'

Tom exhaled harshly and sat up straight. How could she tell something had troubled him? Just like Merle, he thought again. His last foster-mother had always known when Tom had been hiding things. Not physically, but emotionally. Jessica appeared to be as in tune to his emotional status as Merle had been.

Should he tell her? Should he take the risk and answer her question? He looked down into his empty cup, deciding that perhaps it was time he took a small risk. Besides, it might be a good testing ground to see whether or not Jessica *was* trustworthy.

'When I was almost sixteen, I was accused of…sexually harassing the daughter of my foster-parents. She was eighteen years old and the biggest prima donna I've ever met.' Tom met Jessica's gaze squarely as he spoke. He'd been completely innocent and a victim of a bitter and twisted girl's idea of revenge.

'Renee—that was her name—made several passes at me. I ignored them all.' Tom raked a hand through his hair in frustration. 'Perhaps I should have told her straight out that I wasn't interested. In a small way, I was flattered. I mean, I'd seen enough of the seedy side of life to know exactly what she was offering and I was…well…rather advanced in the maturity stakes for my age.

'I'd been with the family for three months before she tried anything. It was little things at first, walking around with her robe open, waltzing through the house from the bathroom to her room with a skimpy little towel around her, gesturing with her body that I should follow. Then she became more blatant, sitting next to me at the dinner table and placing her hand on my thigh as we ate.

'It all came to a head the day I walked into my bedroom after school and found her lying naked in my bed. I told her to get out before I stormed back out of the room. Her mother came home from work and…well, let's just say that Renee distorted the truth completely and my foster-parents chose to believe her rather than me.'

Jess's eyes widened in disbelief. She could see the hurt and pain in Tom's eyes and knew that even today, even though it had been almost twenty years ago, he was still troubled by what had happened back then. Her heart lurched and she wanted to cross to his side and wrap her arms about him. She wanted to kiss away his hurt, as she would a child's.

'That's when you fled the State,' Jess whispered and Tom nodded. 'I don't blame you.' She felt close to him. 'Thank you, Tom. You didn't need to tell me, you know.'

'I know.' His gaze softened and he smiled. 'I wanted to.' Amazingly enough, as he said the words out loud he found that he really meant them. That was a first. Was he really testing her? He wasn't so sure now. She'd believed every word he'd said. She wasn't questioning him now, she was…accepting him.

It was unusual for him to share such deeply emotional parts of his life with a woman, especially one he'd only known for five days. Still, as he'd recognised before, there was something about Jessica that was different. It was instinct and he'd learned long ago to always trust his instincts.

Jess's mobile phone rang and she checked the display. When she didn't answer it, Tom asked, 'Your sister?'

'Yes.' Jess checked her watch. 'I'm surprised she's calling this early. Usually after a Friday night she's not awake until close to evening.'

'You don't like her.'

'She's not one of my favourite people.'

Tom shook his head. 'But she's your sister.'

'So? I didn't choose to have her for my sister.' Jess put the phone beneath the beanbag, knowing Linda would try three or four times to get hold of her.

He watched her carefully and sipped his coffee. 'Is your sister older than you?'

'No.'

'And your brother?'

'He was younger.' Jess looked away. 'He was nine years younger than me.'

'How did he die?' Tom's words were soft and gentle.

'Muscular dystrophy. He was thirteen and the bravest kid I've ever known.'

'You still miss him.' He made the statement as though he knew exactly what she was feeling, and Jess stared at him.

'He's the reason I want to specialise in paediatrics. My inspiration. How about you? Do you have any siblings?'

'No. My parents committed suicide together when I was two.' Jess didn't miss the vehemence in his tone. 'I went from one foster-home to another but things simply went from bad to worse.'

Jess nodded. 'Somehow,' she said softly, 'we manage to pick up the pieces of our lives and go on.'

Tom nodded in agreement. 'When I was sixteen I was placed in yet another foster-home, but this one was different. They were older than my other foster-parents and because they'd never been able to have a family of their own they'd been fostering children for well over two decades. They were the people who helped me sort out my life. If it hadn't been for them...' Tom trailed off. 'They used to help out at the shelter and other foster-homes so when they died I just kept on doing it. When I qualified as a doctor, I offered my services free.'

'So why didn't you want Harley taken to the hospital last night?'

'He'd been missing since Thursday morning. We received a report from the police that he'd run away from his foster-home and they were looking for him. He only needs one more arrest for theft and he's going to gaol.'

'Which is the one place he shouldn't be going to,' Jess agreed. 'He just darted out in front of that car, Tom. If it had been going any faster, he'd have sustained further injuries and possibly even died. As it was, he was a very fortunate boy.'

'You can say that again.'

'What will you do if he *has* been doing something illegal?' Jess finished her bagel.

'I like to uphold the law,' he stated. 'Immediately, though, he's not up to being questioned. I want him to rest and get better.'

'Sounds sensible.'

'Any more questions?' he asked, his smile returning and his hand reaching for a Danish pastry.

Jess felt the full effect of his smile. 'Not that I can think of, but I'll let you know if one springs to mind.'

'Well, I have a question for you.'

Her gaze locked with his, wondering what he was going to ask. As far as she was concerned, they'd already been talking about topics that were quite personal and ones she usually didn't discuss with her working colleagues. Then again, Tom seemed to be pushing the boundaries between colleague and friend.

'Hmm?'

'Why don't you have any furniture?'

Jess laughed, the tension easing out of her. 'Because I move so often. I only have this place leased for another three weeks.'

'Why? Surely they could make it longer. Your contract at the hospital is for six months.'

'I know, but I asked for a six-week lease initially.'

'Why?' he asked again.

'Well…I was hoping to find somewhere, you know, a bit closer to the hospital and I guess it's habit to ask for short leases.'

'Why?' His tone was incredulous. 'This is a great apartment and it's not all *that* far from the hospital. Just contact the agent and ask if you can sign for longer.'

'Don't tell me what to do, Tom.' Her tone held a hint of warning. Jess crossed her arms, feeling very defensive. After being raised by a dictatorial man, there was no way she'd tolerate anyone else treating her in the same fashion.

'It was only a suggestion.'

'Well, I don't need your suggestions, thank you.'

'You're overreacting, Jessica.' Tom watched her thoughtfully as she clenched her jaw and ground her teeth together.

'So?'

Tom took a deep breath, cooling the temper inside that had started to bubble. 'So why is it habit to ask for short leases?'

'You wouldn't understand.' Jess began, her own tone relaxing a bit.

'Try me.'

Jess was reluctant to tell him, not sure he'd understand. 'I usually ask for short leases so I can…well…avoid my family.'

'Why on earth would you want to do that?'

At his accusatory tone, Jess felt her anger begin to rise again. 'Because they're constantly annoying me. My sister has a habit of just turning up on my doorstep, expecting me to drop everything and to go out partying with her. Even if I'm on call! One time, she turned up at the hospital while I was in with a patient and demanded we go out for lunch.' Jess shook her head as the memory returned.

'They don't like the fact that I work. That I choose to have a life without them. I keep a post office box so in an emergency they can post me something. I don't move as often as I used to and once I've left here I'll probably get a lease for the rest of my time in Adelaide.'

'So you're planning to leave the State?'

'Sure.'

'Just to *avoid* your family?'

'See I knew you wouldn't understand.'

'You're right. I don't.' Tom started to pack up the food, screwing the lid onto the Thermos with force. 'Do they live close?'

'No. They live in Cairns.'

'Isn't that far enough away? Adelaide to Cairns is like from Glasgow to Athens!' Tom stood and paced around the room. 'How much further away do you want to move?'

'What's so wrong with wanting to move?'

'What's so wrong with staying in the same place?' he countered.

Jess stood as well and met his gaze squarely. 'If I stayed in Adelaide, it would give my family just one more excuse to bug me. They'd probably buy a house here and spend their summer holidays annoying me while I was trying to work.'

'But they're your family.'

'So? I didn't ask to be related to them, Tom. You don't know anything about the situation.'

'Tell me.' He stopped pacing and stood in front of her, his hands planted firmly in his denim pockets. 'What was your childhood like, Jessica? Was there never enough food to feed you and your siblings? Were all your clothes hand-me-downs that never quite fitted?' Tom watched her expression carefully as he spoke, his fingers clenched tightly beneath the cover of his pockets. He'd endured those things and much more.

'Neglect and abuse come in many guises,' she countered. 'My father had a private investigator follow me around for the first few years after Scott died, and all because he didn't want me to tarnish his reputation. My parents don't take an interest in me because they *care*, Tom. They do it for their own personal gain.'

'What does your father do?'

Jess was steaming now. 'Oh, so now you want to know the details! Well, it's just too bad, Tom. You talked about trust before and the fact that people have to earn your trust—well, the same goes for me. If you're going to start throwing your weight around and questioning me, you can just forget any thoughts you might have about pursuing a relationship with me.'

'What makes you think I want a relationship with you?' he persisted, his tone as vehement as hers.

'Are you blind? The attraction between us is impossible to miss. I didn't ask for it and I'm sure you didn't either, but it's there and there's nothing we can do about it.' The words were out before she could stop them. Jess clamped a hand over her runaway mouth. Any anger she might have felt towards Tom disappeared in an instant.

Tom gazed at her as he unclenched his hands and withdrew them from his pockets. He'd been almost mesmerised by the way her green eyes had sparkled with life as she'd argued with him. Now, though, they held a hint of despair as well as an apology. He felt himself relax as the intense moments they'd shared slipped away. 'You're right,' he acknowledged as he took a step closer. 'There's nothing we can do about it.'

His blue eyes, which had previously been accusing, were now filling with desire. It caused the butterflies in her stomach to circle around each other with such intensity that Jess felt queasy with excitement. She parted her suddenly dry lips as she watched him come nearer. He reached out a hand, his fingers brushing hers lightly before he continued his way up, his fingers warm on her arms until his hands settled on her shoulders.

'Jessica.' Her name was a caress on his lips and her eyelids fluttered closed in anticipation of his kiss. She could feel his breath on her cheek as he came closer still. Her breathing had increased dramatically, and if he didn't make his move soon Jess felt as though she might hyperventilate.

When his lips brushed against hers, Jess sighed with longing. His hands moved around her back and gathered her to him, their bodies pressed against each other. Jess slid her arms around his waist, enjoying the warmth of him.

His kiss was soft and sensual, taking Jess's breath away. Never had any man kissed her in such a way as this. Tom made her feel treasured and cherished. All this from a simple kiss. He opened his mouth slightly and Jess followed suit. When his tongue gently caressed her lower lip, she knew she was lost. Lost in the storm of pleasure and passion that was Tom Bryant.

His teeth nipped at her lip and Jess shivered in delight. As though by mutual consent, they deepened the kiss, each of them seeking a response that both were willing to give. The scent of his aftershave combined with the fresh soap scent from her shower became a heady concoction surrounding them. They held each other so tight, their desire so potent, that for a moment Jess thought she might stop breathing.

Tom groaned as he pulled his mouth from hers, his breathing ragged. He held her tight, burying his face in her neck as both of them tried to regain control. 'Jessica.' He pressed his lips to her neck and worked his way up towards her earlobe where he gently nipped with his teeth. 'You're incredible.'

Jess chuckled, enjoying the feelings and sensations he evoked within her. For this instant, she was happy. Happier than she'd been in a very long time.

CHAPTER FIVE

JESS'S mobile phone rang again. The contentment bubble burst. Jess felt Tom's arms loosen their hold on her as though the phone had brought him back to reality. The reality being that he didn't agree with her methods of dealing with her family.

Without looking at him, Jess stepped from his arms, stalked over to her phone and checked the number on the display before answering the call. 'Just a minute, Linda.' She buried the phone beneath the beanbag.

She turned to Tom who was gathering up his stuff. 'I'll leave you to your call,' he said.

Jess forced a smile, feeling a little unsure of what would happen next. 'OK.' What had she been expecting? Moonlight and love songs? Happy ever after? She hardly knew the man but, she rationalised, she knew him better now than she had five minutes ago. She knew he was the most amazing kisser. She knew he could evoke such a strong reaction within her that it made her want to forget everything.

'Get your research project done and I'll see you bright and early on Monday morning.'

Jess nodded and walked with him to the door. 'Here are your keys,' he said, and placed them in her hand, his warm fingers brushing her palm.

'Thanks.' Jess went to pull her hand away and was surprised to find it held firmly within Tom's. He tugged her closer and she instinctively raised her mouth to his. His lips were perfect, she thought as he pressed them to hers once more. She was overjoyed at this good-bye kiss and she revelled in the brief moment of pleasure, knowing she'd need it to keep her going for the next few days.

'See you on Monday.' His voice was husky and his eyes showed his desire.

She nodded. 'Let me know if there's any change with Harley,' she called as he headed for the lift.

'Will do.' He waved once more as the lift doors opened and he stepped in. Jess sighed with longing and reluctantly closed her door.

'Gorgeous, gorgeous man,' she said, and did a little dance around the room. She collected up the food and placed it on the kitchen bench, switching the kettle on while she was in there.

She packed up the picnic rug and moved the beanbag, only then remembering that her sister was still on the phone.

'Hi, Linda,' she said, her tone cheery.

'About time you remembered I was waiting.'

'Sorry,' Jess apologised. Not even Linda's bad temper was going to bring her down today.

'What took you so long?'

'I was in a meeting,' Jess replied. Well, it was true—even though she hadn't planned it. A breakfast meeting with Tom and now Jess was hoping there would be more of them in the future.

'You still could have taken my call.' Linda's tone changed from dictatorial to sweetness and sunshine. It was the tone she saved for everyone else. 'Guess who I had my picture taken with last night?'

Jess remained silent, knowing that Linda didn't really need her for this conversation. It would take Jess an age and a day to guess and Linda would simply become impatient with her.

'George Dooley!' Linda continued, as though the name was supposed to mean something to Jess. 'He's so gorgeous on television but even more gorgeous in person. We met at…'

Jess felt herself tuning out, allowing her mind to wonder about the man who had somehow become very important to her in such a short space of time. At least Tom hadn't denied the attraction between them. In fact, Jess was extremely glad he hadn't—not after *that* kiss. She fanned her face in remembrance and sighed.

'Jessie? Jessie?' Linda's demanding tone brought her back to earth with a bump.

'Huh? Sounds exciting,' Jess replied, not at all sure what her sister was on about.

'Oh, it was. He's taking me out tonight as well so I'll call you tomorrow with all the details. I wore a new Armani and it looked breathtaking on me. Everybody said so. Mummy and Daddy were there as well, of course, and Daddy said I was the apple of his eye. Then, just before we left, some imbecile of a waitress spilt a drink all over my skirt. She completely ruined the outfit and I had the maid burn it this morning. Of course I had the girl fired, even though she *claimed* it was an accident. It's just not good enough. I don't care if she has ten children to feed. If she's not competent enough to carry a tray of drinks without spilling it, then she shouldn't have a job at all.'

'Hmm,' Jess commented when Linda stopped her tirade. She started spreading out her research papers on the floor, knowing this one-sided conversation with Linda could go on for some time. She may as well get some work done.

'Jessie? Jessie?' Linda demanded half an hour later.

'Hmm?'

'You're not listening to me again, Jessie. Don't you think I can tell when you tune out? You're probably preoccupied with your work, but I'm your sister, Jessie. I deserve your attention.'

'Sure,' Jess answered. She knew the only reason Linda would be remotely interested in what was going on in her life would be if she told her about Tom and the kiss they'd just shared. However, as Linda had made a point of stealing every single man Jess had ever dated in the past, she'd grown used to not volunteering any information about her own love life. Then again, in the past three years she'd only been out on two dates and both of them had been absolute disasters.

'I don't even know why I bother calling you, other than you're my sister,' Linda continued, back on track again. 'In fact, most days I can't believe we're related. I was telling George darling last night that I didn't have any siblings and loved being an only child. That's the way it feels anyway. You know, the Hamptons are giving a party some time soon and their parties are always the best. You should fly up to Cairns and attend.' Jess baulked for a second, amazed at what her sister was saying. 'I've got plenty of dresses you could borrow.'

'Are you sure you haven't burnt them all?' Jess couldn't resist asking.

'Oh, Jessie. I'm shocked you should even ask that question. I only burn the ruined ones.'

'Ever heard of dry-cleaning?'

'Don't be so impertinent. Of course I have. I get all my clothes dry-cleaned.'

'Except the ones that you burn.'

'If I hadn't burnt it, I doubt the waitress would have lost her job. It was the fact that she'd ruined my dress due to her own incompetence that was the deciding factor. The manager even had the gall to inform me that the employee's record had been exemplary. So that's why that dress had to be burnt.'

Jess sighed, unable to believe they were related! If their parents hadn't over-indulged Linda as a child, perhaps she might have been less insipid as an adult. As it was, Jess had worked hard at hiding the hurt she'd felt during her childhood, knowing that her parents favoured her younger sister.

Linda had been an adorable baby, right from the second she'd been born. As a toddler, her blonde hair had been pure white and with her wide blue eyes she'd turned heads wherever she'd gone. Nothing had changed and Linda had lapped up all the attention. Jess's bright red hair, lifeless green eyes and teeth that had needed correcting with braces had made her feel very much the ugly duckling for most of her life.

Tom's words sprang to her mind. He'd said she'd been described as being as tall and as stunning as a model. Even though it had been hospital gossip he'd been quoting, there was no denying that he found her attractive—as other men had in the past. It was just that when they met Linda, Jess knew she paled in comparison.

It was all right—now. She'd proven to herself time and time again that she wasn't in a competition with Linda and sometimes she even felt sorry for her sister. Linda was forever trapped in a mould that would be extremely hard to break out of.

Now Linda was suggesting she come home for one of the Hamptons' parties. The idea was laughable but Jess made herself another drink and nibbled on a Danish pastry while listening to her sister for a few minutes.

'You really should come home for this party, Jessie. You know the Hamptons are a very influential family and it's good business for Daddy to be seen mixing with them.'

'I don't know what my roster will be but I tend to work most weekends.'

'You're always working,' Linda accused.

'That's because I have a job. Besides, why do you need me? You've done without me for the past seven years. I'm sure you'll get by.'

'Jessie, Sean's come home.'

At the mention of Sean Hampton, Jess felt chilled to the

bone. Sean had been her first high-school crush. With his blond good looks and winning smile, she hadn't been the only girl to have had a crush on him. 'So?'

'So he looks *really* good, Jessie. I really think you should—'

Jess had had enough. 'Sorry, Linda, but I need to go. I have a ton of work to get through and I'm already way behind schedule. Bye.'

Jess hung up and sighed heavily. Her earlier happiness had disappeared into a cloud of suspicion. It wasn't like Linda to invite her to a party. In fact, Jess couldn't recall a time when such a request had been made. She wondered how her parents felt about it but then realised that they'd probably put Linda up to it in the first place. Hadn't her sister just said how much she liked telling people she was an only child?

The fact that Sean's name had been mentioned was enough to raise her hackles. For years both sets of parents had talked of Sean and herself getting married some day. 'No.' Jess shook her head. 'Something is definitely brewing.'

On Monday morning, Jess arrived at work bleary-eyed and exhausted. 'Not a good way to start the day,' she mumbled as she helped herself to a much-needed cup of coffee. Nevertheless, her research project was finished and in the post. She sank down into a chair and closed her eyes. To help pep herself up, she'd worn her favourite suit, which was a mixture of earth colours from the outback in Central Australia—the red of Ayres Rock, the green of gum leaves and the yellow of wattle flowers. She'd bought it because it had made her feel relaxed and today she desperately needed to unwind from the pent-up pressures of her weekend.

'You look horrible,' Tom's deep voice said from the doorway to the tearoom.

Jess opened her eyes and smiled at him. 'Thanks for the compliment.' He looked incredible. He wore navy trousers and a chambray shirt. His tie had a well-known cartoon character on it and his stethoscope was slung around his neck. Jess felt her pulse rate increase and worked hard to control it.

She wondered whether she should tell him that the cartoon character depicted on his tie was the same one that adorned the underwear she was currently wearing. She smiled to herself, still a little unsure of what was happening between them. The A and E staff tearoom was hardly the place to strike up a conversation about her underwear!

'Did you eat breakfast this morning?' As he poured himself a cup of coffee, Jess started to realise that he wasn't in a good mood. She glanced at him, noticing that his back was ramrod straight.

'Yes,' she replied, trying to keep a lightness in her tone. 'I finished off the last croissant.'

'Wasn't it stale?' He turned to face her and Jess saw a spark of anger flicker in the blue depths.

'I froze the leftovers,' she explained. She wanted to ask him what was wrong but the more she watched him, the more she realised that he wasn't just angry in general. Tom appeared to be angry with *her*!

'Research all finished?' Tom came to stand beside her before leaning against the table, his legs crossed at the ankles. Even when he was angry, he still looked incredibly gorgeous.

'Yes—thank you.' Regardless of how good he looked, his clipped tone and haughty attitude were starting to strike sparks off her own temper.

'Good. I'm glad it's done.' He was silent for a moment. 'How's your head?'

'Fine.' Jess didn't feel the need to embellish.

'No recurrence?'

'No.' There was an awkward pause between them before Jess asked, 'What about Harley? How's he doing?'

'He's recovering well.' Tom's jaw clenched and Jess felt her impatience rise.

'Is he still at the shelter?'

'Yes.'

'And the police?'

'Why all the questions, Jessica? You already know the answers.'

'What?' Jess frowned up at him. 'What are you talking about?'

'The fact that you just couldn't leave things as they were. On Saturday evening the police turned up, wanting to talk to Harley.'

'So?'

'So how do you think they found out he was there?'

Jess worked hard to control her temper as she slowly stood to face him, their gazes level. 'If I were looking for a missing child, your shelter would be one of the places I'd check.'

'They said they'd received a tip-off that he was there.'

Realisation dawned. 'And you think *I* tipped them off,' Jess stated angrily.

'There were only a handful of people who knew, Jessica.'

'And because I'm the new kid on the block you automatically suspect me? How could you, Tom?' She turned and took her cup to the sink. Jess washed and dried it before turning to face him. 'For your information, I did not contact the police regarding Harley's whereabouts. I may not have agreed with you in keeping him out of the Social Services system, or the fact that the police weren't notified before you operated. However, I also respected your decision. Harley's well-being, both physically and emotionally, was of more importance than arguing with you. But as I'm new, you probably don't believe me now either.'

'Jessica—'

'Don't!' She could see the apology in his eyes but she didn't want it. The fact that he hadn't trusted her—*believed* that she would betray him in such a way—hurt more than she'd imagined. She headed for the door but Tom reached out a hand to grab her arm. She glared down at his hand and he instantly let go.

'Jessica, I'm sorry.'

'Oh, so you believe me now?'

'Yes. I'm sorry I jumped to conclusions. It was just when the police said they'd received a tip-off…' He reached for her hand and gave it a little squeeze. 'I told you that I don't trust easily.'

'That's still no excuse, Tom.' Jess felt her anger vanish in the light of his heartfelt apology. She sighed. 'I know we're still getting to know each other but hopefully you'll at least give me the benefit of the doubt if something like this ever happens again.'

All she wanted now was for Tom to tug her closer and press his lips to hers, showing her that he would try to trust her. Instead, he nodded and dropped her hand. 'So did the police get to question Harley?'

'Yes, under my strict guidance. It turns out Harley has a valid alibi for the break-ins they wanted to question him about.'

'So he's safe?'

'Yes. Hopefully, he'll be in with a new foster-family by next week and that should bring a bit more stability to his life.'

For a moment, they stood staring at each other. Neither made a move. It would be easy to just lean in a little and press her lips to his, but as she was unsure of his reaction she stayed still, her gaze remaining locked with his.

'Jessica…about Saturday,' he said eventually, his tone filled with doom.

'What about it?'

'I don't want you to get the wrong impression.'

A lump started to form in her throat. The way Tom had kissed her good-bye had left her feeling as though he'd wanted to pursue a relationship with her. Now, in the light of reality—or, in other words, the hospital—he'd obviously had a change of heart.

'Really, Tom. Explanations aren't necessary,' she said briskly. 'We shared a couple of kisses.' She shrugged nonchalantly. She was about to say more when a movement in the doorway caught her eye and she turned to see Nicola heading in their direction. Jess took a step away from him.

'Good morning,' Nicola said cheerfully to both of them. 'How did the research project go, Jess? All finished?'

'Absolutely.' Jess was desperately trying not to let her real emotions show through as Tom turned on his heel and walked out the door.

'I had the most fantastic weekend,' Nicola volunteered.

'I'm glad to hear it. What happened?' Jess asked. Yet as Nicola told her about some family party she'd attended with her husband and kids, Jess found her thoughts turning to Tom. Why should she be surprised? Throughout the entire weekend, from the moment he'd left her place on Saturday, all she'd done had been to think about him. It had been extremely difficult to force her mind to concentrate on the research project, and if she hadn't had the unextendable deadline of this morning, Jess would have gladly procrastinated her time away by thinking about Tom.

Now it seemed as though he'd been having second thoughts. Did a relationship with her scare him? He'd told her that it wasn't easy for him to trust people but, hey, she could identify with that. They were very similar in a lot of ways, neither of them making long and lasting friendships or pursuing any real romantic involvement. Then again, she didn't really know Tom all that well. Perhaps she was just deluding herself by thinking they were alike.

When Nicola stopped for breath, Jess took the opportunity to excuse herself. 'I'd better go and see some patients before Tom accuses me of talking all day long,' Jess said with a smile.

'Oh, sure. I'll catch up with you later,' Nicola replied.

Jess went and spoke with one of the nurses. 'Where do you want me?'

'Nose or ear. Which would you prefer?'

'Give me the ear one first,' Jess replied, and took the patient file, scanning it quickly.

'Cubicle eleven.'

'Not a problem.' Jess went to cubicle eleven and found a little girl of four whose ears were very painful. 'Has she vomited?' Jess asked the mother.

'Yes. I tried to get her into my local doctor this morning but they were full so they suggested I bring her here.'

'Did she have a temperature then?'

'Yes. I gave her some child paracetamol about an hour ago.'

Jess felt the little girl's forehead. 'She's still quite hot. Hello, Megan. I'm Dr Jess. I need to have a little look in your ears. Will you try and keep really still for me?'

Megan nodded and Jess smiled. 'Good girl. First of all, I'd like to take your temperature again.' Jess picked up a tympanic thermometer. 'This is a fancy new gadget,' she told Megan. 'If I just put it in your ear for a few seconds...' Jess was demonstrating as she spoke '...then when it beeps...' the thermometer beeped '...it means it's ready and—look at that.' Jess pointed to the small screen that displayed the readout of Megan's temperature. 'Those numbers tell me that your temperature is a bit higher than normal but I'm sure it'll come down again soon. Now, though, I'm going to have a look inside your ear. We'll just get Mummy to come and sit up here on the examination bed...' Jess waited while Megan's mother did so. 'And, Megan, if you could sit on Mummy's lap then she can help hold your head nice and still for me.'

Jess showed Megan's mother how to effectively hold her daughter to ensure the four-year-old stayed still. If she moved suddenly, Jess might accidentally hurt her with the otoscope. 'See this little light?' Jess showed Megan the otoscope. 'This shines a light right down your ear so I can see what's going on. Here we go,' Jess said, and had a look. 'And the other side.' Once Jess had taken a look in both ears, she checked with Megan's mother to see whether she was allowed to have a lolly. Her mother assented.

'Here you are, Megan. What colour would you like?'

'Pink,' she replied, and dutifully helped herself to a pink lolly from the jar.

'Both of her ears are quite red, which indicates they're infected—nothing to worry about, though. She has otitis media, which is quite common in children her age. It's a condition that affects the middle ear when infection gets in through the Eustachian tube. A course of antibiotics should clear it up. Also, try to keep water out of her ears while they're healing.'

'So she'll be all right?'

'She'll be fine.' Jess smiled at her patient.

'I was just so worried when she started vomiting. It's not like her. At first I thought it was something she'd picked up from pre-school but she kept pulling on her ear as well.'

Jess wrote out the prescription. 'As I said, she should be fine. If her temperature persists for more than forty-eight hours, she should see someone again—either bring her back here or take her to your local doctor. Keep up the paracetamol for at least the next twenty-four hours until the antibiotics start to work.'

Jess gave Megan's mum the script. 'Come on, sweetie.' Megan's mum held out her hand to her daughter. 'Let's say goodbye to Dr Jess.'

When they'd left, Jess wrote up the notes and placed it in the clerks' box. She was at the nurses' station when she saw Tom bringing a patient through.

'Jessica, I'll need your help,' he said as a girl was wheeled into triage room two. Jess followed him and two of the nurses. 'Ashlee, this is Dr Jessica. She'll be here to help as well,' Tom said to his listless patient who was being hooked up to an oximeter as well as an ECG machine.

'Hi, Ashlee.' Jess scanned the notes. Ashlee was nine years old and according to her parents had been losing weight during the past week. They'd seen their local doctor on a few occasions who had performed different tests but had never really explained what he was doing. This morning, however, Ashlee had been complaining of abdominal pain and she'd vomited twice. The sputum had been yellow and blood-streaked. Not a good sign. She'd been restless and slightly confused. Jess noted that Ashlee's breathing was rapid and deep with a fruity smell on her breath. Her skin turgor was abnormal, indicating dehydration.

'She's going to be all right, isn't she?' Mrs Arlington asked as she sniffed into her handkerchief. Mr Arlington placed his arm about her shoulders, murmuring soothing words.

'We're going to do everything we can to help Ashlee,' Tom promised. 'All right. I want oxygen by non-rebreather mask and obs.' The nurses started to carry out Tom's orders. 'Jessica—complete blood picture, please. Check the glucose levels immediately and I want a complete work-up to check the bicarb levels and the anion gap.' He turned to the parents again. 'When was her last food intake?'

'Last night.'

'Thanks.' He turned to the nurse. 'Obs?' he asked.

'Increased pulse, tachycardic and respirations are high, BP is down, blood-sugar level is twenty-two point three,' one of the nurses reported.

Jess had finished taking a blood sample. 'Get this over to the lab marked urgent,' she said to one of the nurses who had just finished using the glucometer to give them an immediate readout of Ashlee's glucose levels.

'Urinalysis,' Tom ordered, before checking the child's oxygenation and the ECG readout. He felt Ashlee's abdomen.

'Skin's dry, lips are dry, extremities are cold,' Jess reported, as Ashlee groaned.

'Sorry, darling,' Tom soothed as he finished palpating her stomach.

'Eyes are sunken,' Jess remarked. 'Breath has a slight acetone odour. Mrs Arlington, what did your local doctor suspect was wrong with Ashlee?'

'At first he said it was just puberty and growing pains. The next time he thought she might have anorexia, which I thought was silly because she was still eating her food, and the third time he told us it was a viral infection and there was nothing we could do but just ride it out.'

'Why?' Mr Arlington asked. 'What do you think?'

'Is there a family history of diabetes?'

'Uh…' Mrs Arlington gazed up at her husband before looking back at Tom, her eyes wild with uncertainty. 'I'm…I'm not sure. Not that I know of. Why? Is that what you think is wrong with her?'

'We need to do a few more tests to confirm this, but at the moment I think it's diabetic ketoacidosis.' He turned to one of the nurses. 'IV saline bolus 200 mils over twenty minutes. Insulin, fifty units.' He checked the oxygen saturation levels and the ECG readout again. 'Hopefully, we'll see a change soon enough.'

'Keto what?' Mrs Arlington asked as she looked helplessly at her daughter.

'Ketoacidosis,' Tom repeated. 'Diabetes is an imbalance between glucose and insulin levels. Insulin is responsible for carrying glucose through the blood so it can be broken down and utilised for fuel. With the absence of insulin, the muscles become deprived of fuel and the glucose accumulates in the blood. It's then excreted through the urine and takes a lot of water with it. This causes dehydration, which is why we're getting fluids back into Ashlee right now. We need to do this slowly otherwise we'd have other complications to deal with.'

Mr and Mrs Arlington nodded and Tom continued.

'Because the muscles aren't getting enough fuel, they consume it from the protein and fats instead. This causes the muscles to waste and a dangerous acidic compound called ketones are formed. This becomes a condition called diabetic ketoacidosis.'

'And this is what Ashlee has?' Mrs Arlington asked, her voice a quivering whisper.

'Yes.'

'So the weight loss was her muscles starting to waste?'

'Yes.' Tom turned his attention back to his staff. 'Obs?'

'Pulse is strengthened slightly. Breathing still laboured.'

'How are you feeling, Ashlee?' Tom asked the girl softly. She opened her eyes and gazed at him but closed them again.

'Is she OK?' Mrs Arlington asked again.

Tom smiled at them. 'She's going to be fine. She responded to my voice which means she can hear us, but at the moment I think she's just a bit too exhausted to exert much effort.'

'S so we d-did the right thing to bring her in,' Mrs Arlington stuttered. 'I felt so foolish, bringing her to the hospital, but I didn't know what else to do. I didn't want to take her back to that doctor again.'

'You did the right thing,' Jess confirmed.

'Absolutely,' Tom agreed. 'Get someone from Endocrinology down here, now that she's stabilising,' Tom instructed the nursing staff.

'Will Ash need insulin injections?' Mr Arlington asked.

'Yes,' Tom replied. 'There are two types of diabetes and Ashlee has type one, which can be controlled by insulin.'

'Oh, no.' Mrs Arlington shook her head, her husband's arm tightening around her.

'We'll put you in touch with a representative from the diabetes association,' Jess told them. 'They'll be able to explain things to you and help you get set up at home. There are support groups for families as well as for the people who suffer from it.'

'I know it seems like the end of the world at the moment, but even at this stage Ashlee is responding well to treatment,' Tom told them. 'Once the endocrinologist gets here, he'll take over her treatment as he's a specialist in this area. She'll be admitted to hospital for a few days and will probably be in CCU—Critical Care Unit—for a few days.'

Tom checked the readings from the oximeter and ECG once more and was glad to find no abnormalities. When the endocrinologist arrived, Ashlee was transferred into his care and the Arlingtons thanked both Tom and Jess profusely.

'And now for the nose,' Jess said as she walked towards the nurses' station and picked up the notes. Tom had been wonderful with Ashlee and her parents. He was a terrific doctor and even in just the way he was around the patients, she knew she'd be learning a lot from him. It was another facet of his personality and she was trying to fit it in with the other areas he'd given her a glimpse of.

He had no family. He'd been helping out in a homeless shelter since he was a teenager. He'd had an unfair accusation of sexual misconduct levelled at him. He found it difficult to trust people but with his patients he was caring, kind and, oh, so giving. How could a man who had been through so much in his life be such a giver when hardly anyone had given to him?

'Are you going to use mental telepathy to read the notes, Jessica?' Tom's droll tone asked from behind her.

Jess clenched her teeth, cross with herself for being caught daydreaming. Still, it would have looked funny—her standing in the middle of the corridor, glaring at a closed file. She turned to face him. 'I tried to but it didn't work. Guess I'll have to open the file after all.'

'What's the case?'

'Marble up the nose.' She wrinkled her own nose as she spoke.

'You don't like noses?'

She shrugged. 'I like them better than eyes.'

'You're not into getting things out of people's eyes?'

'Only if I really have to. Everyone has a queasiness about something. What's yours?'

Tom looked up and down the corridor before leaning in closer. 'Redheads,' he said softly. 'I deal with them only if I absolutely have to.'

Before Jess could figure out whether or not he was joking, he'd turned on his heel and walked away. She closed her eyes and counted to ten, now desperate to get him out of her mind so she could concentrate on her work.

In cubicle three, she found the seven-year-old boy who'd managed to shove a marble up his nostril. She was able to extract the obstruction with minimal complications but a lot of screaming from the child. For a moment she thought back to darling little Robbie who'd required sutures in his head and hadn't made a sound.

She smiled at her patient, knowing this was just his way of expressing himself. His main reason for pushing it up there in the first place had been because he'd wanted to see if it would fit.

'Please, try not to stick things up your nose any more. It really isn't very good for you and next time you might really damage your sinuses.'

He promised he wouldn't and was happy to get his marble back. Jess wrote up the notes and decided that she really needed a cup of coffee before seeing anyone else. As she sipped at the brew, she reflected on Tom's comment. His queasiness was to do with redheads. Was this his polite way of warning her off? Telling her she was getting too close?

Frankly, Jess didn't think Tom would let any woman close enough to see the real him—the real mushy man deep down inside—but if he ever did…At that moment, how she yearned to be that woman.

Even just admitting this to herself, Jess felt helplessly vulnerable. This was the beginning of her fifth week of being in Adelaide, her fourth week at the hospital and her second week working with Tom, and somehow, in that short time, her life had been tipped sideways. The question was, how did she stop it?

'There you are,' a female voice said from the doorway, and Jess sat up straight in her chair. 'Remember me from the other night? Kathryn, the orthopod?'

'Of course.' Jess smiled.

'How are you feeling? Did that migraine take hold? You should have said something sooner.'

Jess shrugged. 'It didn't really hit me until after we'd finished operating. Coffee?'

'No. I have a meeting in five minutes but just thought I'd stop by and see how you were.'

'That's nice. Thank you.' Jess was genuinely touched.

'You're welcome. Jack and I would like to have you around for dinner some time. It's organising our diaries that's going to be the hard part, but I'm sure we'll manage it somehow.'

'OK.' Jess was surprised. Usually, work colleagues didn't go out of their way to get to know her. Perhaps Kathryn was different. 'Let me know what date you're thinking about and I'll check my roster.'

'Sounds good.'

'Uh, Kathryn.' Jess stood and faced the other woman. 'It's not a, well, set-up…or a blind date or anything like that?'

'No.' Kathryn shook her head, her auburn braid swishing

from side to side. 'Although we will be asking Tom. Trying to co-ordinate four doctors' schedules should be an absolute nightmare but hopefully we'll have you around some time before Christmas.' She laughed.

'So Tom and I would be the only single people there but it's not a set-up,' Jess reasoned.

'My kids will be there,' Kathryn told her matter-of-factly. 'They're both single.'

Jess smiled. 'Oh, well, that's different, then. I don't suppose either of your children are in high school?'

'Not yet, but our son Mitchell starts next year. Listen, it would be a very informal dinner, more a gathering of friends.'

'Does Tom know that you've invited me?'

Kathryn placed both hands on her hips, a smile twitching at her lips. 'I don't need to tell Tom Bryant *everything* I do. That honour I reserve for my husband.'

Jess laughed. 'And rightly so.'

'Now I'd really better get going or Jack will shoot me for being late for yet another meeting.' With that, Kathryn left the tearoom. She also left Jess's mind buzzing with another load of what-ifs regarding Tom.

CHAPTER SIX

JESS had just finished her coffee when one of the nurses came into the tearoom. 'Electrocution patient coming in,' she said, and Jess rushed out to the waiting room to see a little girl being wheeled into triage room one.

'Three-year-old girl—electrocution,' Belinda said as Tom came in as well. 'Not quite sure exactly what happened, but patient is alert and coherent.'

'Hello,' said Tom, speaking to the little girl. 'What's your name?'

'Kelly.' The word was barely audible.

'Kelly,' Tom repeated. 'That's a most beautiful name. My name is Dr Tom. We're going to lift you onto this big bed now, Kelly, so we can take a look at you.' Tom tenderly touched her cheek. 'Have you been crying?' Kelly nodded. 'Oh, dear. You must have had such a fright.'

Jess came over with the ECG cables. 'This is my friend, Dr Jessica.'

'Hello, Kelly.' Jess smiled. 'You have lovely curly hair, don't you? My hair is straight and hardly ever curls.'

The girl nodded.

'See these funny circle things? Well, these are pads that I'm going to put on your chest and that way we can see what your heartbeat is doing,' Jess explained, before lifting the little girl's top up and doing as she'd said.

'How old are you, Kelly?' Tom asked.

'Free.'

'Wow. What a big girl. Have a look at this funny thing. It's like a big bandage. I'm going to wind this around your arm so we can keep a track of your blood pressure and that will let us know how you're feeling. All right?'

Again, Kelly nodded. 'Good girl.' When that was done, Tom turned to the nurse who had taken a statement from the parents.

'She'd been jumping on a couch and grabbed a wall-mounted light with her left hand. It came off the wall. The electric shock sent her flying across the room. She then started to scream and cry.'

'I would, too,' Tom remarked. He picked up her left hand and took a look. Jess looked closely as well. Her hand looked as though she'd taken a black paintbrush and coloured her hand with stripes, her index, middle finger and thumb being the worst. Still, it wasn't very sore to touch and was more like a stain than dead skin.

'Still some copper filings from the light in her fingers,' Jess murmured, and Tom nodded.

'I put her hand under cold water,' Kelly's mother said. 'I hope that was right?'

'Perfect,' Tom told her. 'That has definitely helped her hand not to blister. All right, Kelly. I'm just going to feel your tummy and have a listen to it with my stethoscope. Just lie back for me—that's a good girl.' Kelly smiled as he touched the little girl's tummy. 'Is that a bit ticklish or are my fingers a bit cold?'

'Tickle,' Kelly replied.

'That's a good sign. Let's have a listen now.' While Tom listened to Kelly's abdomen, Jess checked the ECG and BP readings.

'Good.' She turned to the parents. 'Did she have these shoes on…' she pointed to the running shoes Kelly now wore '…when the accident happened?'

'No. She had bare feet,' her mother replied.

'Kelly, I'm just going to take your shoes off so I can have a look at your feet.' Jess was looking for entry and exit wounds. 'Your feet look fine,' she remarked a few seconds later. They checked the ECG readings again, watching closely for dysrhythmias.

'We'd like to keep her in for a few more hours and see how she goes,' Tom told her parents. 'At this stage everything is quite routine for electric shock and Kelly seems to be recovering. What I'll do next is get those copper filings out of her hand and fingers, but after that her hand should heal in no time.'

'Thank you,' Kelly's mother said with a watery smile as she hugged her daughter. Jess checked with Tom that he didn't require her assistance any more, before leaving him to it.

The day continued to move along at a steady pace but even so Jess didn't manage to get a lunch-break until after two o'clock. Just before five-thirty, she went into the changing rooms where she kept her coat and bag. The door burst open and a nurse came in, sniffing and crying. Jess recognised her as one of the new nurses who had started in A and E that morning. From what Jess had seen, she'd made a few mistakes, which was common when you weren't sure where things were.

'What happened?' Jess asked, and the woman looked up, obviously thinking she'd been alone.

'Nothing.' She sniffed again and opened her locker.

Jess shrugged her shoulders and took her coat out.

'I don't think I can work in A and E. Not if the director is going to treat me like an imbecile. I've heard the gossip about him and how difficult he is to work for.'

OK, Jess thought, realising that the woman did want to talk about it. 'You mean Tom?'

'Yes. He just took me aside into his office and told me to be more careful with what I was doing. It's my first day,' she wailed. 'I can't help it if I'm not Miss Perfect all the time. Besides, who is he to tell me off?'

'He's the Director of Accident and Emergency,' Jess replied.

'But I'm a nurse. He's a doctor.'

'I have no doubt that Tom spoke to your nursing superior before he discussed things with you.'

'You think so?' The nurse seemed horrified.

'Yes.'

The nurse's gaze narrowed. 'I should have expected as much from you. You're a doctor. I thought you might understand, being a woman, that some days we just don't feel well.'

'Is that what the problem is?' Jess asked.

'Yes. I'm bloated and cramped and—'

'And generally feeling miserable,' Jess finished. 'Still, you're at work and when you're here, although it's difficult, you have to put your personal problems aside and focus on the patients. If you're not feeling well, you need to go home and rest.'

'But this happens every month. I can't keep taking a day off work every month just because I have my period.'

'If things are that bad, I suggest you see a doctor about your cycle.'

'I don't need a—'

'Just because you're a nurse, it doesn't mean you don't need a bit of help from time to time. There are natural remedies to help control bloating and cramps. There are hormonal treatments. You do have choices and it's up to you to be responsible and find out which ones are the best for you.'

'Still,' the nurse said, 'he could have cut me a little slack. It's my first day!'

'I think he has cut you some slack. Just because you're a woman and you have PMS, that doesn't mean you get special treatment. As a nursing professional, it's the right of your superiors to demand a lot of you, especially when you're dealing with other people's lives. There's no room for slip-ups.'

'Yeah, I guess,' the nurse said resignedly.

Jess grabbed her bag and closed her locker. 'So, will we see you tomorrow?'

'I'm not rostered on until Wednesday evening.'

'Hopefully, you'll be feeling a bit better by then.' Jess made her way out of the changing rooms, just wanting to get out of the hospital and head home. It had been an emotionally draining day, which had had nothing to do with the patients or her work. She thought about what she'd said to the nurse and knew at times it was difficult to just push your personal problems aside, but if she didn't, the patients wouldn't get her full attention—and they deserved every bit of it.

For Jess, today, thinking about Tom and working with him since they'd shared those kisses on Saturday had been a lot harder than she'd anticipated. To top it all off, it appeared as though he'd wanted to apologise for them and that was the last thing Jess wanted. Right now she wanted to lock those sensations and memories up. That way, she could take them out and relive them whenever she was feeling down—or masochistic!

Tom was standing at the end of the corridor. 'Did that nurse go into the changing rooms?'

'Yes.' Jess yawned and smiled apologetically.

'Is she OK?'

'Yes.'

'You look worn out,' he said softly.

'I feel worn out.'

'Come into my office for a few minutes, please. I want to talk to you.'

'Oh, so it's my turn to cry now, eh?'

Tom grinned wryly at her as they walked past his secretary's empty desk and into his office. He closed the door behind them. 'Are you going to tell me I was wrong to speak to her? That I shouldn't have made her cry?'

'You didn't make her cry, Tom. She allowed herself to

cry. From what she told me and from what I witnessed myself today, you were right to speak to her.'

Tom seemed amazed. 'You agree with me?'

'Yes.'

'Did you tell her that?'

'Yes.'

He eased down into his chair.

'What's the matter?' Jess asked as she sat.

'Nothing. I'm just…amazed.'

'Why? Don't your registrars usually back you in what you say?'

'Ordinarily they just talk about me behind my back,' he said matter-of-factly.

'Well, I'm not like that.' Jess insisted.

Tom gazed at her, the atmosphere between them changing from one of business to one of pleasure. His smile was sexy and Jess felt its full effect as a small shiver washed over her. 'So I'm beginning to notice,' he drawled, his tone husky with repressed desire.

Jess was hypnotised by his eyes and for a split second forgot to breathe. Her gaze flicked from his mouth to his eyes, the sensations of anticipation spiralling throughout her body. Her mouth became suddenly dry and she parted her lips, allowing the air to escape.

He was a handsome man—fact. She was attracted to him—fact. Now what?

He cleared his throat and shifted in his chair. 'Jessica…' he began, and then stopped. He stood and walked around his desk to stand in front of her.

Jess started to rise, not wanting to hear the words he was more than likely going to say. She didn't want him to apologise for kissing her. She wanted to remember that morning in all its splendour, without adding to it the memory of him apologising for his behaviour.

Tom leaned forward to try and stop her from standing, but he was too late and they accidentally bumped heads.

'Ow,' they both groaned, their hands instantly rubbing the contact spots. Tom took her hand as she tried to move away.

'Please, Jessica.'

'No, Tom.' She stopped him and squared her shoulders, hoping she'd be able to say this and look him in the eyes. 'I don't need any explanations.' Her gaze met his and for a brief second she faltered. 'Let's just continue to work together and keep our relationship professional.'

Tom dropped her hand like a hot potato and stared at her. 'If that's what you want,' he said finally as he shoved his hands into his trouser pockets. He turned and walked back behind his desk.

'No!' The word was out before Jess could stop it. Had she read the signals wrong? She'd been sure he'd been about to apologise. 'Please, continue, Tom. I shouldn't have interrupted you.'

'It's fine.' He clenched his jaw.

'Come off it, Tom. We're both people who prefer to speak their minds rather than tiptoe around on eggshells. I really am sorry that I stopped you just now.' Jess looked down at her hands. 'It's not what I want, Tom.'

'Then why did you say it?'

'Because I thought you were about to apologise for kissing me on Saturday and I couldn't bear to hear you say it had been a mistake.'

'I was going to apologise,' he replied, and Jess felt her stomach churn. So she hadn't read the signals wrong.

'Then…?'

'Jessica, I was going to apologise for kissing you because I've never kissed another member of my staff. I usually keep my distance, as you've heard, but with you…' Tom broke off and raked an unsteady hand through his hair. 'With you…I'm drawn to you,' he finished with a shrug. 'I have no idea how things will go but I think we owe it to ourselves to find out. I've only known you for a week, and already I've opened up more to you than I have to any other woman—in a romantic light, of course.'

Jess smiled at his words. 'I know what you mean. I usually keep pretty much to myself, but with you…' She took a step closer to him, edging around his desk. 'Well, I find myself drawn to you as well.'

'I'm sorry about this morning,' he said again, but Jess placed her finger across his lips, silencing him.

'It's all right.'

Tom reached for her and pulled her into his arms, bringing them face to face. She usually wore shoes with a small heel, but even with the extra height from them she was still a little shorter than him. A first!

'I've never dated a woman this tall before,' he remarked quietly.

'I've never dated,' she replied.

Tom pulled back and looked at her in astonishment. 'What?'

'Not in the true sense of the word,' Jess explained. 'I'd go out with a guy two or three times and then my sister would swoop down on the helpless prey and carry him away.'

'And you let her?'

'They weren't worth fighting for.'

'So do you want to?'

'Do I want to what? Fight for you?'

He chuckled. 'No. Date.'

'You?' Jess pretended to think it over. 'Hmm. You come with an awful lot of baggage.' She looped her arms about his neck.

'From what I can tell, so do you,' he replied.

'Then again, we could classify my non-existent dating experience as a…*challenge*…that needs your expert guidance.'

Tom nodded, his smile increasing. 'Of course, and as

your boss, I did promise to help…*strengthen* those areas
that were in need.'

'I guess it's all settled, then.'

'I guess it is,' he replied. 'Let's seal it with a kiss.'

'What a good idea.' Jess's eyelids fluttered closed and
she sighed with happiness as Tom gathered her closer, his
lips pressing firmly to her own.

At the knock on his door, both of them sprang apart
instinctively. Tom reached for her hand. 'No, Jessica. If
we're going to do this, we're not going to hide it.'

Jess pulled her hand free with a laugh. 'All right, but we
don't need to flaunt it either.'

'Good point,' he answered, before calling, 'Come in.'

The door opened and Dirk Robertson walked in. He
looked from Jess to Tom and back again. 'Can't you two
control yourselves for one moment?'

Tom raised his eyebrows while Jess tried hard to smother
a giggle. Here they were, just agreeing to begin a relationship, completely forgetting the hospital had had them
matched up a week ago.

'Did you want something in particular, Dr Robertson, or
do you just like making idle comments and walking out?'

'I'd like to discuss next week's rosters,' he replied.
'And…and to apologise for my comment just now. It was
completely inappropriate of me.'

'Apology accepted,' Tom said. 'Take a seat.' He turned
to Jess. 'I'll call you later.' He made no effort to kiss her
but the way his gaze encompassed her made her
feel…special. She knew this would be another bit of information Dirk could add to his gossip list but right at that
moment Jess felt too wonderful to even care. Tom wanted
to date her! What more could a girl need?

Jess smiled at him and, after collecting her coat and bag,
left the two men to talk over the rosters. As she walked out
of Tom's office, Nicola passed by.

'Hi, Jess. How's everything going?' The urology registrar inclined her head towards Tom's office.

'Fine,' Jess said, hoping that the silly I'm-ecstatically-happy grin was off her face, but she could tell by the twinkle in Nicola's gaze that it wasn't.

'So should I still not listen to everything I hear?'

Jess laughed as she put her coat on and the two women headed off to the doctors' car park. 'Personally, I'd say don't listen to the gossip at all—or, at least, don't put too much importance on it.'

'But you and Tom are dating, aren't you?'

Jess laughed again, remembering that the hospital grapevine was well ahead of their actual relationship. 'We're seeing each other,' she confirmed.

'Fantastic,' Nicola replied. 'It's about time Tom let someone through those barriers.'

'How long have you known him?' Jess was now becoming quite curious about the man she hadn't been able to stop thinking about.

'Quite a while, actually. It was Tom who first got me interested in medicine. That's why I'm forty-one and still a registrar.' Nicola smiled. 'Still, one more year and I'll be finished my training.'

'Good for you,' Jess replied heartily. 'I admire people who set themselves goals, and—applaud them when they reach them.'

'Thanks.'

'You're most welcome.' Jess found that the more she got to know Nicola, the more she liked and respected her. They stopped at a car and Nicola pointed.

'This one's mine.'

'I'm over there. I'll see you later,' Jess said, and started to walk off.

'Jess?' Nicola called, and Jess retraced her steps. 'Go slowly with Tom. It's been quite a while since he dated.'

Jess smiled. 'So I gathered, but as I've never really dated much I guess that puts us on a more even footing.'

'Really?' Nicola was surprised. 'But you're so... gorgeous. I imagined you with a string of boyfriends, all of their hearts breaking wide open.'

'No. I leave that type of shallow relationship to my sister.' She bit her tongue, angry with herself for saying too much. 'I'd better go. Thanks for the chat, Nicola.' Jess waved and headed over to her Jag before she said anything else about her family.

There wasn't much she could do about it now, she thought as she drove home. She'd said what she had on the spur of the moment and she'd be wise to remember to hold her tongue next time.

At home, Jess prowled around her apartment. With her research project done, she now felt at a loose end. She flicked on the radio but couldn't get interested in the talk-back discussion, and as she didn't own a television she didn't have that medium to distract her.

After she'd had a shower and made herself a sandwich, Jess spied her balloon-making kit sitting in a plastic bag by her bedroom door. 'Perfect.' In next to no time, she was pumping up balloons and twisting them into animals. She did a giraffe first and then decided to tackle her defunct imitation of a poodle.

'Still not as good as Tom's,' she told it. She went into her bedroom and collected the poodle he'd made for her on Saturday. She'd kept it by her bed, along with her giraffe.

Four more tries and she thought they were starting to improve. By the fifth attempt, she jumped up in jubilation. 'Yes!' She looked at the bubbly little dog and, after finding a marker pen, drew a face on it. 'Tom is going to be so proud,' she told the balloon, and then laughed at how silly she must look. She was happy.

She glanced at her mobile phone, sitting on the bench,

willing it to ring—willing it to be Tom. He'd said he'd call her but she had no idea what that really meant. Would he call her and ask her out for an official date? Would he just call to chat? Would he call tonight or another night?

'No wonder I don't date,' Jess told the poodle. 'It's just too much trouble.' She glanced at the clock. Eight-thirty. She didn't have Tom's home number and although she could call the hospital switchboard and ask them for it, she didn't want to stir up any more gossip than necessary.

'The shelter.' She looked at the poodle. 'He'll be at the shelter.' Running on excited anticipation, Jess grabbed her coat and keys and headed out the door. She came back in a few seconds later and grabbed the poodle as well. She wanted to show him, to share her accomplishment with him. It was a strange feeling.

The only person she'd ever had that feeling with before had been Scott. He would have loved to have seen her twisting balloons into all sorts of contorted shapes. He would have laughed at all her attempts while still encouraging her to continue.

Jess tenderly placed the poodle on the passenger seat before heading in the direction of the shelter. After she'd pulled up outside and parked her car, she started to have doubts. Perhaps it wasn't a good idea to come. What if Tom wasn't here?

'You're here now,' she said out loud. Without giving herself time to think about it again, Jess climbed out of the car, holding the poodle firmly in her hands just in case the wild, wintry wind whisked it away.

She faltered once more after pushing open the double doors as the front entrance was devoid of people. Should she walk through? Should she call out? Should she wait? A whole minute ticked by and Jess felt her heart rate increase with anticipation and anxiety. She turned to face the door and was on the verge of walking out when someone said her name.

'Hello, Jess,' Clarissa welcomed her warmly. 'How are you feeling, dear? Tommy told us all about your migraine, you poor thing.'

'I'm fine, thank you.'

'Nice balloon. Reminds me of the ones Tom does. Well, what can I do for you? You haven't been looking for any other children tonight?'

Jess smiled. 'Uh…no. Actually, I was…um…wondering if, er, Tom was around.'

'He is, dear. Come through with me.' Clarissa turned and led the way down a corridor, one that was vaguely familiar to Jess from the previous Friday night. They went past the infirmary to the end, and when they got there, instead of going right as they'd done previously, they went left. 'He's just saying goodnight to the children.'

'Oh? I didn't realise you had children staying here all the time.'

'It depends. Some nights we have a lot sleeping here and other nights it's only a few. It all depends. Most of them are placed in foster-homes but some manage to dodge the system and have no place to go. It's too cold to sleep outside in winter and as they know they won't get pressured here, they feel comfortable coming inside for a meal and a bed.'

Clarissa stopped beside another door. 'If you'll just wait here, I'll go through and get him. I'd invite you in but it might put some of the children on guard and I don't want them getting razzed up when it's high time they should be sleeping.'

Jess could hear muffled noises coming from the other side of the door, and when Clarissa opened it she gasped in surprise, her hand automatically coming up to cover the smile on her lips.

'What?' Clarissa mumbled as both she and Jess gazed at a room full of beds, devoid of pillows. Boys of all ages were everywhere, throwing pillows and hitting each other with them, and in the middle of them all was…Tom.

He'd changed out of his suit into a pair of old jeans and a jumper. His hair was completely messed up and his mouth was curved into the widest smile she'd ever seen. His deep chuckles blended with the laughter from the boys and Jess thought she'd never seen a more welcome sight.

She glanced at Clarissa who was having a hard time keeping a straight face, but she persisted in her role of 'mother'. She stood silently at the door, her foot tapping impatiently on the floor.

One of the boys caught a glimpse of her and the laughter immediately died from his face. It was like a chain reaction, watching each boy become aware that they'd been discovered, the laughter disappearing into thin air.

Finally, it was only Tom's rich laughter that filled the room, and when that died down he, too, looked towards the door, his gaze encompassing the two women who stood there.

'Thomas Andrew Bryant,' Clarissa said as she took a few steps into the room. 'What on earth do you think you're doing?'

Tom stood and grinned down at her. 'What does it look like?' he asked. 'We're having a pillow fight.' With that, he brought the pillow in his hand up to land squarely on Clarissa's arm. 'Defend yourself,' he challenged.

The room was frozen. No one moved and everyone appeared to be holding their breath. Jess knew she was. Everyone was waiting for Clarissa to make a move.

With lightning speed, she whipped the pillow out of his hand and thumped it right onto his head.

The boys in the room hooted with laughter as they all joined in. Jess simply stood at the door and laughed, a warm fuzzy feeling filling her entire body. These children, who had so little, still had the gift of laughter and it was enough to help them forget their worries for a while.

She watched as Tom was attacked from all sides and could see how much he was enjoying himself. These children were his family, she realised, and it made her feel happy to know that, even though he'd obviously been through so much, no one had ever broken his spirit.

Her heart swelled with the warm fuzzy feeling, knowing Tom's actions and attitude only endeared him to her even more. He was an amazing man and Jess could feel herself become more attached to him as time went on.

Deciding she'd better leave him to it, Jess headed back down the corridor and into the dining room. She placed the poodle on a table and went to stand in front of the heater. She shouldn't have come. This was Tom's special place where he came to relax and unwind, as well as fulfill his need to help people.

She envied him. Throughout her life, the only special place she'd had had been her imagination. That was one reason why she'd moved so often—because she was trying to find the place where she *really* belonged.

As a child, she had withdrawn from her family and their meaningless talk, preferring to read books. One after the other. She'd devoured everything in her father's library and then started searching out books of her own. Medical books had always intrigued her, and after Scott had been diagnosed they'd intrigued her even more.

'Jessica.'

Even the way he said her name made her feel all gooey and mushy inside. No other man had ever evoked such a reaction within her—ever! She turned slowly to look at him, wondering what his reaction might be to her just arriving here at the shelter.

'Hi.' He looked gorgeous. His hair was still messy in places even though he'd tried to finger-comb it back into place. Jess felt her heart turn over in delight.

'Is everything all right?' He crossed to her side.

'Yes.' She reached out and picked the poodle up off the

table. 'I was excited,' she said as she showed him the balloon animal. Even though she felt completely silly, Jess knew her trip here hadn't been completely wasted. She'd been allowed to catch another glimpse of the real Tom Bryant, and those glimpses were becoming more precious than anything else.

'Hey.' He smiled and took it from her. 'Well done.'

'I'm sorry to just barge in when you're…you know…here with the children but…' She shrugged. 'I was so excited and I wanted to…share that with you.'

Tom gazed at her and slightly shook his head. Then he put the balloon back on the table and tenderly placed his hands on either side of her face. He brought his mouth to hers, capturing her lips in a long and sensual kiss. 'Thank you,' he whispered, and rested his forehead against hers. 'I'm pleased that you wanted to share your excitement with me.' He took a deep breath and reluctantly eased back.

Jess smiled at him, feeling less silly than before. 'I'll…um…let you get back to the children.'

'OK.'

'OK,' she repeated, and pulled her coat tightly around her. 'See you tomorrow.' She turned and headed towards the door.

'What about your balloon?' he called.

Jess spun around, her gaze drinking him in. 'It's for you.' She blew him a kiss. 'Bye.'

Tom watched her go with a mixture of emotions. Even after the outer doors had closed, he still stood there, looking down at the purple poodle she'd made. He'd never had a woman give him such an extraordinary gift—or a more precious one. Jessica had wanted to share her accomplishment and excitement and she'd chosen to share it with him.

He took another deep breath, really filling his lungs. Jessica Yeoman was so completely different from every other woman he'd been involved with during his life and, truth be told, it was starting to scare him a little.

CHAPTER SEVEN

JESS parked her car and was heading up to her apartment when her mobile phone rang. She checked the screen—it was her mother.

'Jessie, darling,' her mother crooned after she'd answered the call. 'I'm glad I caught you. There's something I'm just desperate to discuss with you. I know Linda called you the other day and told you about a party the Hamptons are having,' her mother continued, without even letting Jess say a word. 'Well, it would be just perfect if you could come to it. Your father has arranged a plane ticket for you.'

There must be something very important happening to her father's career if they wanted her home this desperately.

'Jessie? Jessie, are you there?' her mother asked, when Jess didn't immediately respond.

Jess closed her door and took a deep breath. 'I'll have to check my roster. I work most weekends.'

'Well, ask for the weekend off. It's going to be the most splendid party and everyone will be there. You won't want to miss it.'

'I'll see—but chances are I'll be working.'

'Jessie, I don't know why you even need to work at all. Besides, I'm sure there are other people who can do the work for you.' When Jess didn't say anything her mother rushed on. 'Please, come, Jessie. It will be so wonderful to have the family back together again.'

'Why is it so important that I come to this party?' If there was one thing Jess knew her mother didn't like, it was being confronted head on. She doubted whether she'd get a truthful answer but it was worth a try.

'I've told you why. It would be nice to have the family

altogether again and the weather up in Cairns is so beautiful.'

'Oh. In that case, I'll schedule some time off and come
home—'

'Good girl,' her mother interrupted.

'After Christmas,' Jess continued. 'You don't seem to
understand that I have less than five months left of my
registrar training. My work means a lot to me—more than
a silly party. So, for the last time, I will not be coming.'

'But, Jessie,' her mother persisted, but Jess had had
enough. She disconnected the call. Tears stung her eyes.
How dared her family try to make her feel guilty? How
dared they try to pressure her, saying they wanted a family
reunion? She'd been feeling so happy, so completely on
top of the world, and in a matter of minutes the desolation
she'd carried around with her for years had returned.

Couldn't they see that she wasn't like them? That she
wasn't interested in money, power or fortune? She was different from them and they didn't like it. Her father hadn't
liked it that Scott was different and so he'd privately denied
ever having a son. He'd even gone as far as accusing her
mother of having had an affair—Scott being the product.
Why her mother had stayed with him after that Jess had no
idea, but eventually they'd sorted things out.

At first they'd wanted to put Scott into a home—to keep
him out of the way. Jess had fought them on that—and had
won. Then her father had begun to realise that having a
disabled son could help his political career. His attitude had
made her sick. He'd be out advocating the rights of the
disabled whilst behind closed doors ignoring his only son.

After her father had agreed to let Scott live at home, he
hadn't spoken another word to him. Indeed, he'd hardly
spoken to Jess and she was sure he'd been as relieved as
she'd been when she'd finally left the family home.

So it was just a little hard for her to believe that after
seven years of never hearing a word from her father, he

suddenly wanted to play happy families again. No. There had to be something really big happening at the Hamptons' party and they needed Jess there to win.

Her head begin to pound and Jess knew she had to stop thinking about them. She took some paracetamol to stave off a repeat performance of her migraine, and went to bed. She focused her thoughts on her patients, on her balloon animal accomplishments and on Tom.

The memories of his kisses were definitely keeping her warm and she was certainly becoming addicted to them!

'So, how are things going with Jess?' Nicola asked Tom two weeks later.

'Good,' he replied as he wrote up another welfare report on one of the children who'd recently been at the shelter. The child in question had been successfully placed with a foster-family and Tom hoped that she would be happy there.

Nicola rose from the chair and walked over to peer out the window into the dark night. 'She's different, Tom.'

'I know.' Still he didn't put down his pen. He knew Nicola wanted to talk. The thing was, Tom wasn't sure whether he wanted to discuss his relationship with Jessica. It wasn't that he didn't like her—it was quite the opposite.

'How many of your little ''tests'' has she passed now?'

Tom slammed down his pen and glared at her. 'Nicola, I'm trying to get some work done here. I don't want to discuss my relationship with Jessica.'

'Why not?'

'Because I don't.'

'Come on, Tommy. Who else do you have to discuss women with other than me? I'm the closest thing you have to a sister, and trust me, you definitely need some sisterly advice right about now.'

She'd captured his attention and he had to give her points for effort. He eased back in his chair and crossed his arms defensively in front of his chest. 'What makes you say that?'

'I know you, Tom. Probably better than most people. I've lived your past, remember. I just wish we'd both been with Alwyn and Merle at the same time.'

'Yeah. It would have been fun to have had an ''older sister'' around. I could have teased you.' He grinned.

'Oh, yeah. Usually it's the older siblings that do the teasing, not the younger, but by the time Alwyn and Merle took you on I was long past childhood.'

'A whole seven years, Nicola.'

'It may not be much difference now but back then it certainly was. You were sixteen and I was twenty-three.' Both were silent for a while. 'I still miss them,' Nicola said softly.

'Me, too.' Tom reached out and briefly squeezed her hand. She *was* the closest thing he had to a sister and he was glad they'd stayed in contact over the years.

'And if Merle were alive today, she'd be as pleased as Punch to meet Jess.'

Tom groaned and rolled his eyes. 'Back on this topic?'

'Ah…you thought you'd successfully diverted me.' He nodded. 'I'm not that easily sidetracked, Tom. So, what are you going to do about it?'

'About what?'

'About where your relationship is heading.'

'We're taking it slowly, Nicola.'

'I can understand that, but where's it going to end up? Look, Tom, I love you. Regardless of the fact that we're not related by blood, you'll always be a little brother to me, but I like Jess—a lot. You can't afford to play with her emotions. Don't lead her in one direction only to veer off at the last minute because you're too scared of a personal commitment.'

'Who said I'm scared?'

'Aren't you?' Nicola asked tenderly.

Tom wasn't sure what to say. He wasn't sure he wanted to face these facts just yet. He needed more time.

'I've been down this road. When I met Travis, it was the most scary and fantastic thing, all at the same time. We took it slowly, as you know, and it took a lot of courage to step forward and grasp a new life—a new beginning with him. Now look at me. I'm forty-one, married with two children and pursuing a career as a urologist. *Me*—a doctor! Life is so unbelievable, Tommy, and I need to make sure that you're grasping it with both hands. Good things *do* happen to people like us, people who were rejected as children. There *is* love waiting for us out there so if that's what you think you might have found with Jess, please…' She took both of his hands in hers. '*Please*, Tommy, don't let her get away.'

The phone on his desk rang and he disengaged his hands. 'Dr Bryant.'

'Hi.' Jessica's voice washed over him like a tidal wave of happiness. 'Busy?'

'Not really. I was just chatting with Nicola.'

'Nicola Muir?'

'Yes.'

'Was there an emergency? Are the children all right?'

He smiled. 'Everyone's fine. Nicola is, well, sort of like…' Tom looked at the woman he was talking about. She was grinning from ear to ear and giving him a thumbs-up sign. 'My big sister.' There was silence on the other end of the phone. 'Jessica?'

'Yes? Sorry, you've kind of taken me by surprise. How can she be sort of your big sister?'

'We were raised by the same foster-parents, although by the time I was taken in by Merle and Alwyn, Nicola had already left. We've stayed in contact ever since.'

'I see. That would explain her interest in our relationship, then. So, have I passed muster?' Jess was trying to process this new information. She knew they'd both agreed to take it slowly, but surely he could have mentioned something like this earlier? Then again, perhaps it was just another step closer to finding the real Tom. He was a complex man, but she hadn't realised just how complex until they'd agreed to date. On the other hand, who was she to chide him for being reticent in volunteering information? She hardly ever spoke about her family, or the fact that her parents probably wanted her to marry Sean.

'With Nicola?'

Jess detected a teasing tone in his words.

'Nah—she can't stand you.'

'That's not true!' Jess heard Nicola's voice in the distance. 'I'll talk to you later, Jess.'

'No you won't,' Tom protested. 'Don't you need to go home to your husband and family, *sis*?'

She heard Nicola chuckling before she called, 'Goodnight, Jess.'

'Night,' Jess replied, a smile on her lips.

'Jess says she never wants to speak to you again,' Tom relayed.

Jess laughed. 'I didn't say that at all, you lying rat-fink, and you know it.' He was silent for a moment. 'Has she gone?'

'Yes, and for ever, with any luck.'

'You don't mean that.'

'No. You're right, I don't. So, what have you been doing this, your first evening off night shift?'

'Studying—what else?'

'Do you need any help?'

'With the studying?' Jess purred seductively down the phone, and Tom cleared his throat. She laughed. 'No. I'm fine at the moment.'

'Are you rostered on tomorrow?'

'What? He who writes out the roster hasn't memorised when I'm on?'

'Well, I must admit that I have taken a particular interest

in what days you're working, but I didn't think you knew,' he admitted, and she laughed again. Tom enjoyed making her laugh. He'd never realised how much pleasure he could get by making someone else—someone he really cared about—happy. 'How would you like to do something different after work?'

'Sure, but won't you be at the shelter?'

'Yes, but I'd like you to come, too.'

Jess was stunned. She'd discovered that Tom had a small one bedroom—shack was the only word for it—out the back of the shelter. Jess had been aware that the children and staff there were his family and she hadn't wanted to intrude. During the past two weeks, depending on what shift she'd been on, she and Tom had basically spent time together at work, often eating the midday meal together, as well as going out the couple of free evenings they'd shared, but never had he asked her to come to the shelter with him.

'Er…are you *sure*?'

'Yes. I think it's about time you really got to meet my "family".'

Jess felt a knot begin to tighten in her stomach. If Tom wanted her to meet his family, that could only mean that he was interested in meeting hers. Couldn't it? 'Ah…of course. I'd love to come,' she heard herself answer, and wondered what she'd got herself in to.

'Great. It'll be fun.'

'Can we have a pillow fight?' Jess asked, hoping he wouldn't mention her family.

He chuckled. 'I don't see why not. Listen, Jessica, I have a ton of work to get done so I'll say goodnight and sweet dreams.'

'See you tomorrow.' As she hung up, Jess realised that Tom was taking their relationship to the next level. Was that what she wanted? Would she ever get up the nerve to introduce him to her manipulative family? Would she want to?

The next morning Jess woke up feeling exhausted. 'Not a good way to start the day,' she told her reflection. She dressed and drove to work, arriving just before seven o'clock. By midday she'd seen a steady stream of patients but no sign of Tom. He was probably at a meeting or working in his office but, still, even just the sight of him would have revived her flagging energy.

After lunch, a four-year-old boy was brought in by his father. Jess read the notes the triage sister had taken and gave the boy a thorough check-up. Young Alex had managed to get into the medicine cabinet and had drunk a bottle of liquid paracetamol.

'I wasn't sure what to do so I brought him in,' the father commented. 'He usually goes to day-care during the day— I'm a single father,' he added. 'But as he wasn't feeling too good, I took the day off work.'

'What time did you give him paracetamol?' Jess asked.

'Just after nine o'clock this morning. He had a temperature all night and the clinic sister I spoke to said to keep him dosed up on paracetamol for twenty-four hours or until his temperature went down.'

Jess looked at little Alex, lying on the hospital bed. He was drowsy, which was to be expected. 'Can you remember how much was left in the bottle? Was it half-full?'

'It was a new bottle.'

'Two hundred mils?'

'Yes.'

'How much was left in the bottle?'

'Not much.'

'All right. We'll do a blood test to confirm the diagnosis but it's pretty certain he's swallowed quite a bit so we'll get him started on treatment.'

'What's that?' Alex's father asked as he smothered a yawn. 'Excuse me,' he apologised. 'It hasn't been an easy night.'

'Of course,' Jess replied with a smile. 'The treatment is charcoal.'

'Charcoal? Like out of a fireplace?' Alex's father asked incredulously.

'Yes, although this is activated charcoal which has been treated to increase its absorption. What we do is mix it with water and then get young Alex here to drink it.'

'And that's it?'

'Well, he'll need to stay in overnight for observation but generally, yes, that's it.'

'Oh!' Alex's father sat down on the edge of the bed with a bump. 'I've been feeling so guilty for not locking the cabinet after I put the medicine back in, although I could have sworn that I did.'

'Children of Alex's age are more than capable of putting keys into locks and turning them, as well as getting bottles out of cupboards and opening them. It's an unfortunate accident, but in a few days he'll be back to normal.'

'Creating more mischief,' his father said with a crooked smile.

'Exactly,' Jess replied, and wrote up the treatment plan, leaving it to the experienced nursing staff to carry it out. She returned to the tearoom and made herself a cup of coffee. Still no sign of Tom. She sighed miserably and sat down at the table, leaning forward on her arms to rest her head.

'If you're going to sleep at work, Dr Yeoman, I'll need to report you to your superior.'

Jess's head came up with a start at hearing Tom's voice. 'You're here,' she said, and then realised how silly that sounded.

'Correct.' He had a teasing smile on his lips and Jess found it contagious. 'I'm a firm believer in the philosophy that wherever you go—there you are.'

'Very funny, Tom.' He came and sat beside her. 'Have you been stuck in meetings?'

'And then some,' he groaned. 'How's your morning been?' Tom placed his hand over hers and gave it a little squeeze.

'Busy…but better now you're here.'

Tom smiled, that gorgeous sexy smile she loved. 'Ditto,' he said softly as he leaned over to kiss her. Jess had always felt a thrill of excitement wash over her the instant before their lips met—and this time was no exception.

Whenever Tom kissed her, she felt as though she was safe. As though nothing could ever harm her again. It was a feeling she'd been waiting her entire life to experience. He was so good for her and, she flattered herself, she was just as good for him.

His lips were soft and tender on hers and she felt herself instantly relaxing. 'You're like an addictive drug, Jessica Yeoman,' he murmured against her mouth. 'One I can't seem to get enough of.'

'I know exactly how you feel,' she replied, and he kissed her once more before pulling back and standing up.

'Unfortunately, I need to—'

'There you both are,' one of the nurses said. 'Belinda asked me to fetch you. A four-month-old baby has just come in and Belinda would like you to take a look.'

'Both of us?' Tom asked.

'Yes.' They all hurried back to Triage as the nurse gave them some preliminary details. 'Patient's name is Lachlan Gribble. His mother brought him in because she wasn't happy with her local doctor's diagnosis.'

'Which was?' Tom asked.

'Reflux.'

'He's been vomiting a lot then?' Jess queried and the nurse nodded. If they'd had any doubt as to where the four-month-old was, they only had to follow the loud crying noise that filled A and E. When they reached triage room two, Tom pulled back the curtain that had been drawn around the bed.

'Hello,' he said, raising his voice over the noise. 'I'm Dr Bryant and this is Dr Yeoman. I gather young Lachlan here hasn't been feeling too well today.'

'Nah. Well, actually, it's been goin' on for quite a while now,' the mother told them as she paced up and down with her son in her arms. 'Ever since 'e was born, 'e's been vomitin' but everyone told me that was normal but it's not just like, you know, normal vomitin' and stuff—'e gets it right across the other side the room.'

'Projectile,' Tom said.

'Yeah. I took 'im up to me local doctor and 'e just said it was reflux and that was that.' The mother had tears in her eyes and started to cry. ''E's just been so sick and 'e's not feedin' properly and I'm on me own and I just dunno what else to do and I'm so tired.'

'What's your name?' Jess asked softly as she patted the other woman on the shoulder.

'Sera.'

'OK, Sera. We're going to take a look at Lachlan and see if we can figure out what's wrong with him,' Jess told her. 'Is it all right if I take him from you? Dr Bryant needs to feel his tummy. Come and take a seat up on the bed next to him and we'll see what we can find.'

Sera handed Lachlan over and Jess held the screaming child in her arms. The baby cried even louder as Jess laid him on the bed and tried to stretch out his little tummy long enough for Tom to do a proper examination.

'You said he hasn't been feeding well?'

'Nah.' Sera blew her nose. 'I've tried 'im on a bottle as well as feedin' 'im myself, and anythin' 'e does swallow 'e soon brings back up again.'

'I'd like Dr Yeoman to feel his tummy so she can confirm my diagnosis.'

They swapped places and gently palpated little Lachlan's abdomen. Just at the end of his stomach, she felt a lump about the size of a pea. She continued with the examination but could find nothing else wrong. 'There you go, you poor darling,' she told Lachlan. 'We've finished poking and prodding you for now.'

Jess watched as Tom picked up the baby, cradling him for a brief moment before handing him back to his mother. Now Jess had another image to add to her mental photo album. A picture of Tom holding a baby—and he'd looked *very* good.

'Pyloric stenosis?' Tom asked, and Jess nodded. 'Contact Dr Sommerville.' Tom directed his order to one of the nurses before returning his attention to Sera. He picked up a piece of paper and a pen and started to draw a picture. 'This is the stomach,' he said, and drew another bit coming down. 'This is the duodenum, which is the first part of the small intestine. The area where the stomach and the duodenum meet is called the pylorus. The pylorus is a strong muscled ring that opens and closes, controlling the movement of food. Now, what has happened in Lachlan's case is that this muscle—the pylorus—has narrowed, obstructing the flow of food into the duodenum.'

'But…but how?' Sera's eyes were wide with astonishment.

'It's usually hereditary,' Jess answered.

'It often happens in first-born males and the fathers generally have a history of it themselves,' Tom added.

'So…so what 'appens now? 'Ow ya gonna fix it?'

'The only way to fix this is by surgery. It's a small operation where the pylorus is widened, thereby allowing a free passage of food from the stomach into the duodenum.'

Sera was completely shocked and Jess didn't blame her. For the past four months she'd been told it was normal for her son to be so sick or that it was just reflux. Now they were telling her that her baby would require surgery.

'The paediatric surgeon is on his way to see you and we'll be handing Lachlan's care over to him.'

'So 'e 'as to have it?' Sera asked.

'Yes. Unfortunately, it's quite a common condition. The operation itself doesn't take long and after a few days in hospital he'll be able to go home.' Tom ran his fingers over Lachlan's downy head and smiled. 'After the operation, he'll be even more gorgeous than he is now.'

Thankfully, Lachlan had started to settle and the room was a bit quieter. Jess started to write up the notes ready for the surgeon.

'When will he have the operation?'

'Some time today or tomorrow,' Tom told her, and again the young mother grew quite pale. 'I know it's all quite sudden but, believe me, he needs it. He can't go any longer not keeping down a reasonable amount of food.'

The curtain opened and another man walked in. 'Sera, this is Dr Sommerville, the paediatric surgeon, who will talk to you about Lachlan's operation. He'll be the surgeon in charge.'

Jess and Tom remained for a few more minutes while the surgeon palpated the baby's stomach, agreeing with their diagnosis. After that, Sera was whisked up in the whirlwind of getting her son ready for emergency surgery. One of the hospital social workers came to see her and within an hour Lachlan had been settled in one of the wards in preparation for surgery early in that evening.

The rest of the day dragged on with Tom heading off to catch up on some paperwork while Jess continued to see one patient after another. As five o'clock came, the number of patients in the waiting room usually doubled as people who hadn't made it to their local GPs in time came to the hospital.

By seven-thirty, Jess was drained. She'd been there for over twelve hours and had only managed a few minutes alone with Tom. As she collected her things from her locker, she noticed apprehension and nervousness were starting to set in. She was happy Tom had decided to let her meet his 'family' but was it what she really wanted?

'Suppose it has to happen some time.'

'Hi, Jess. Talking to yourself again?' Nicola asked as she walked into the changing rooms. She headed to her locker and put her coat and bag away.

'Yes,' Jess replied, feeling self-conscious around Nicola now that she knew about the close relationship the urology registrar shared with Tom.

'Relax,' Nicola told her.

'Are you a mind-reader?'

'No, but your rigid body language was speaking volumes. I won't bite, Jess.' Nicola sat down on the bench next to her. 'Anything I can help with?'

Jess smiled. 'Thanks, but I think this is something Tom and I have to work through by ourselves.'

'Relationships aren't easy.'

'Tell me about it.'

'They need a lot of work.'

'You can say that again, but the work needs to be done by *everyone* involved.' Jess had her family in mind while she spoke.

'You sound as though you've been burnt.'

She nodded. 'Very badly, but not in a romantic sense,' she clarified.

'You need to talk to Tom about it,' Nicola urged. 'He's a good listener. I can testify to that. He's always been there for me, especially when I started dating Travis. No, relationships aren't easy and, yes, they need work by all people involved, but the relationship I'm referring to is between you and Tom. You have something special, Jessica. Don't let it get away.'

'Have you said this to him?'

Nicola nodded. 'Basically. You've made him happy, Jess, and for that I thank you. I've only known you for a short time but I've seen a big change in you. Tom's good for you, too.' Nicola's beeper sounded and she groaned.

'The night begins.' She stood. 'Talk to him, Jess. Tell him what's on your mind. I've got to go.'

Jess nodded. 'Thanks, Nicola.'

'That's what interfering surrogate big sisters are for.' She laughed before heading out.

Jess knew that if she didn't go and meet Tom at his office soon, he'd be paging her. After her talk with Nicola, some of her earlier apprehension had eased. *She* knew she and Tom were good together but to hear someone else say it, someone who wasn't in the relationship, made Jess feel more confident.

On the other hand, she also knew that Nicola's advice was right on the mark. She had to talk to Tom about her family but where to start? My father is a manipulative control freak? My mother is a doormat and my sister is a mixture of the two? Not a good introduction.

She pushed the thought out of her mind as she walked past his secretary's empty desk and knocked on his office door.

'Come in only if you're a gorgeous six-foot paediatric registrar who answers to the name of Jessica,' he called, and Jess couldn't believe what he'd said.

'Tom!' she said as she pushed the door open, sped through and closed it just as quickly. 'Don't say things like that.'

'Why not?' He grinned as he put down his pen and came towards her.

'It could have been anyone.'

'No. If it had been anyone else, they wouldn't have been allowed to come in,' he replied as he wrapped his arms about her waist. 'I've had a hectic day and I need my Jessica fix.' With that, Tom gathered her closer and pressed his lips to hers.

Jess wasn't about to argue and slid her arms around his neck. The scent of him enfolded her and she sighed, enjoying the familiarity of him. After a few moments, she pulled back to gaze up into his hypnotic blue eyes.

'Everything OK?' he asked as he stroked his hands in little circles on her back.

'Uh-huh.' She nodded. 'How about you?'

'Better now you're here,' he replied, repeating her words from earlier that day.

'Cute. Very cute.' Jess kissed him. 'What time do we need to be at the shelter?' She eased from his grasp.

'Something's wrong,' he stated. 'Talk to me, Jessica. We've come this far without shutting each other out. Let's try to keep going.'

'It's not easy, Tom,' she whispered.

'I know,' he replied. 'To trust another person by telling them how you feel isn't easy. I remember seeing no less than fifteen child psychologists during my time and all of them were desperate for me to confide in them.'

'I know what you mean.'

'You saw fifteen child psychologists?' he asked, trying to inject a bit of humour into the suddenly sombre atmosphere.

Jess smiled. 'Just one.'

'Why?'

'Because my father thought I needed it.'

'Sometimes parents are wiser than the child.'

Jess backed away and clenched her jaw. 'I was fourteen, Tom, and I knew I didn't need to see anyone. Don't go presuming you know what it was like growing up in my family. You have no idea what it was like in my household.'

'Why are you trying to pick a fight with me?' he asked.

'What?' Jess was flabbergasted. 'Me? You're the one who's antagonistic.'

'It's because I asked you to come to the shelter, isn't it?' he asked rhetorically.

Jess shook her head.

Tom nodded his. 'You think that because I'm letting you meet the people I classify as family, you'll have to reciprocate and allow me to meet yours.'

'Do I?'

'Yes. Someday.'

'I knew it.' Jess turned and headed for the door, but Tom was there before her.

'Someday, Jessica.' He placed his hands tenderly on her shoulders. 'If our relationship is going to progress, we need to take it to the next level. We need to start interacting more in each other's lives.'

'Does your decision have anything to do with what Nicola said to you?'

Tom frowned. 'In a way. She just helped me to confirm some things. Why? Has she spoken to you?'

'Yes.'

'When?'

'About ten minutes ago.'

'What did she say?'

'She told me to talk to you.'

'And will you?'

'I don't know if I can.'

'Do you trust me?'

'It's not that, Tom.' Jess clenched her hands together and tried to get a firm grip on her thoughts. 'Even telling you about my family will…well, it might make you…' She couldn't do it.

'Might make me what?' Tom waited, but Jess only shrugged.

'Oh, I don't know. I feel so silly.'

'You're not being silly, Jessica,' he soothed, and rubbed his hand up and down her arm.

'Well…you might not want to date me any more.'

Tom frowned and stared at her. 'Are they that bad?'

'Yes.'

'Then this is a matter of trust, Jessica. You need to trust

me to make up my own mind. You've asked me to trust you and now you need to do the same.'

He was right. It wouldn't be easy but, then, what other part of her life *had* been? She gazed up at him, her earlier anger dissipating. 'You're right. I was, unconsciously, trying to pick a fight with you so I wouldn't have to go to the shelter this evening. I will tell you about my family, Tom, but just not yet.'

He smiled. 'Progress, Jessica. We're making progress.' He pressed his lips to hers in triumph. 'Just as well we're paediatricians and not psychologists, otherwise our relationship would go in continual circles while we tried to psychoanalyse each other.'

She chuckled and nodded. 'True.'

'Shall we go to the shelter?'

'Yes.' Jess followed Tom in her car, and had a wonderful evening meeting the children and getting to know the staff a little better. The pillow fight was a lot of fun and this time they had it with the girls.

Afterwards, Tom and Jess had talked about a variety of topics that interested them, and just after midnight he walked her out to the Jag.

'I had a fantastic time,' she told him as they huddled together next to her car, the cold August wind whipping around them.

'Me, too. You'll have to come again on your next night off.'

'It's a deal.'

'Shall we seal it with a kiss?'

'Why, Dr Bryant,' she crooned, 'I thought you'd never ask.'

Tom's kiss was as perfect as all the others had been but this time there was a hint of something else. A hint of permanence. Jess secretly delighted in it. As she drove home, careful of traffic, she thought about how important he was to her. Surely it was worth taking the risk and opening up a bit more?

Her earlier exhaustion had disappeared, and after such a wonderful evening she doubted whether she'd be able to get to sleep at all. She dressed for bed, and after she'd brushed her teeth she gazed at her reflection in the mirror.

She wasn't just happy any more, she was ecstatically happy. Tom was…everything.

'Everything,' she said out loud, and as the realisation of her words started to sink in, her expression turned to one of horror. 'Oh, no.' Jess eyed her reflection quizzically again, hoping she was wrong. 'Oh, no,' she groaned again. 'How could you have been so careless?'

Not only was she ecstatically happy, she was also in love. In love with Tom Bryant!

CHAPTER EIGHT

IT WAS hours later before Jess finally drifted off into a restless sleep. At five-thirty, she gave up trying and showered. With excess energy to burn, she cleaned her apartment from top to bottom and started packing things into boxes. By seven o'clock she was back to being exhausted again, but she dressed for work and headed to the hospital.

Tom was the first person she encountered when she walked through the hospital doors. Jess's heart turned over with love and her stomach lurched. The piece of toast she'd eaten for breakfast wasn't sitting too well.

'Good morning,' he said, and studied her. 'You don't look as though you slept too well.'

Jess's stomach lurched again and she realised she'd better move. She rushed past him and into the changing rooms where she was sick. 'This isn't happening,' Jess mumbled as she rinsed her mouth and put her coat and bag in her locker. 'He's going to be worried now.'

He was waiting just outside the door and almost pounced on her when she re-emerged. 'Are you all right? What happened?' He placed his hands on either side of her face and peered closely at her. 'Jessica?'

Jess was touched by his tenderness. 'I'm fine,' she told him. 'Just tired.'

'Have you had any more headaches?'

'Nothing bad. I just…didn't sleep well last night.'

'Are you sure?'

'Well, that and I have to move some time this weekend. Which reminds me, would it be possible to change my shift? I was on days but if I could work Saturday night instead, it would be a help.'

'You're moving? In two days' time?'

'Yes.' They headed down the corridor towards the tea-room. Jess desperately needed another cup of coffee. 'Remember I told you my lease was only for six weeks?' He nodded. 'That's up on Saturday.'

'You've been in Adelaide for six weeks already?'

'Yes. Hard to believe, isn't it?'

'Where are you going to? Have you found another place?'

'Yes.'

'Will you buy furniture this time?' he asked, and Jess laughed as she made them both black coffee, adding sugar to Tom's.

'Perhaps. I'm usually not there enough to need it, that's all. It also makes moving a lot easier.'

'Do you need help packing?'

'No. It's under control.'

'OK, then. I'll see if I can change your shift on one condition.'

'What?'

'You let me help you.'

'It's not necessary, Tom. I don't have that much stuff and it usually takes about two trips with the Jag and it's all done.'

'That's the condition—take it or leave it.'

She sighed and smiled at him. 'All right. You leave me no option. I'll take it.'

'Good.' He pulled her closer. 'Let's seal it with a kiss.'

'You like sealing your victories with a kiss, don't you?'

'Not with everyone,' he responded as he wiggled his eyebrows up and down. 'Just you.' Tom pressed his lips to hers and Jess started to feel better. How was it that a few minutes in his company lifted her spirits and made her feel as though she could fly? It was love, she reminded herself as he pulled away.

Beep. Beep. Beep. Their pagers shrilled in unison. Leaving their coffee, Jess and Tom rushed towards triage room one.

'It's Michael Warden,' Belinda said as she handed Tom the notes. 'Lacerations to the head. One of his friends brought him in.'

'Damn it,' Tom growled and crossed over to the twelve-year-old boy. 'Hey, Mikey. I was hoping not to see you for a while.'

'Dr Tom?' The boy gazed at him through eyes that were only slits.

'Yeah, it's me, mate. We'll wind the bed up so you can rest back on the pillows more comfortably. Then we'll take a look at your head.' While Tom spoke, he checked Mikey's pupils. 'Equal and reacting to light,' he reported. One of the other nurses was taking his blood pressure.

'One-twenty over sixty,' she reported.

'Set up an IV, please.' Tom looked at his patient. 'Mikey? Mikey? Can you tell me what happened?'

'Dr Tom? Is that you?'

'Sure is. Can you tell me what happened?'

'I fell down,' Mikey answered, his eyes closed.

'How did you fall down?' Mikey didn't answer. 'Come on, Mikey. You know you can trust me. Don't go protecting your old man. He's not worth it.' Still no answer. 'Hold still and we'll take a look at your head,' he said.

Jess checked Mikey's reflexes. 'Here.' She held her patient's hands. 'Squeeze my hands.' He did. 'Good.' She reported the findings to the scribe nurse.

Tom checked the boy's pupils again but reported them as still equal and reacting to light. 'Neurovascular obs,' he instructed as he returned to looking at the two gashes in Mikey's head. 'There are bits of glass in his hair,' Tom said as he extracted one. 'Ten mils of midazolam IV. The bleeding has stopped for the moment but we need to get his head cleaned and sutured. Then I want a head X-ray.

Call Welfare and get Sergeant Kedomyer on the phone. I'll speak to him.'

'You want Mikey's home checked out?' Jess asked softly, and Tom nodded. 'So you don't mind Welfare getting involved in this instance?'

'No way. I'd like Mikey out of his ''loving'' home environment sooner rather than later. He's already been in here six times in the last two months with suspicious injuries.'

When the midazolam had started to take effect they started to clean and suture their patient's scalp. Tom and Jess worked very well together and finished the task with care and precision.

'Get him into Radiology,' Tom told the nurse as he pulled off his gloves. 'I'll be in my office. Call me when he's done. Jessica, I'll need you with me when I speak to Welfare and Sergeant Kedomyer. If there's the slightest change in any of his neurological obs, I want to know,' he stated, before walking out. Jess followed him.

'You're a bit hot under the collar,' Jess commented as they walked into his office. Tom shut the door behind them and prowled around the room, his hands clenched into fists at his sides.

'I've been there, Jessica. I've lived the life Mikey and Harley are living. I've been beaten and bruised. I know what it's like to feel like an outsider coming into a ''normal'' family. I've been in street gangs. I've scrounged for food. I've slept in places that would turn your hair green, and all by the time I was fifteen. Then there was the sordid event with Renee.

'I didn't want to talk to anyone. I didn't want to open up, to tell them what was going on. I was afraid of betraying the gang I was in and, believe me, betrayal in a gang carries serious consequences. Trusting someone really doesn't come easily to me and I know how Mikey feels. He doesn't like it that his dad is batting him around and although he wants to tell someone, he's not sure of the consequences if he does. I can understand that.

'What I want to do is to *show* Mikey that I understand. That I'm not going to judge him. That I really am going to help him, to the best of my ability. Yes, I'm hot under the collar and I have every reason to be. Everyone I've ever allowed myself to trust—*everyone*—has let me down at one time or another.'

'Except for Merle and Alwyn.' Her words were spoken softly and Tom stopped pacing. 'Sometimes,' she continued, 'it takes extraordinary circumstances for people to break that code of silence. When did you break your silence, Tom?'

She really did understand him. It was so uncanny it scared him. 'After Renee,' he whispered. 'You think Mikey might be at the end of his tether?'

'I certainly hope so. For Mikey's sake. You had Merle and Alwyn to trust. They sound like the most wonderful people, Tom. Every time you speak of them, your eyes light up. Every child at the shelter looks at you exactly the same way. Mikey looked at you that way.'

'I want to help him.'

'Then help. You make a big difference in the lives of those children at the shelter and I know you'll work just as hard to ensure Mikey doesn't return home again. Keep him in here for the next few days under observation. That'll give Welfare time to investigate a bit more and hopefully find a fost—'

'It's not only that,' he interrupted. 'Even if Mikey gets into a great foster-home, his biological parents can still have access to him. The kid's been in foster homes before, with regular visits from his parents. His father has given him drugs and alcohol which then upsets the routine his foster-family is trying to get him into. Then when the father can prove that he's back on his feet again, Mikey will be ripped out of the foster-home and given back to his parents.'

'What about his mother?'

'His father beats her, too, but I doubt she'll ever leave.'

'But hasn't someone talked to her and told her that—'

'She knows, Jessica. She doesn't want to leave.' Tom turned away from her and walked around to his chair then sat down. 'Alwyn told me that the worst part of fostering was when the real parents stuck their noses in. Sure, occasionally it works out, but nine times out of ten it doesn't.'

Jess sat down in the chair opposite him, feeling quite desolate. She had a lot to learn about this fostering business but she was up to the task. 'If you need me to do anything, count me in,' she offered.

His secretary buzzed through to say that Sergeant Kedomyer was on the phone. Tom took the call and switched it through to the speaker-phone. After introducing Jessica, Tom informed Kedomyer of the situation with Mikey. Jess was amazed at how Tom had stripped all the emotion from his tone. It would do Mikey no good if Tom didn't retain his professionalism at all times. Kedomyer promised to get a police unit around to Mikey's house to check things out.

As soon as he'd finished with the call, the welfare people arrived and together they discussed immediate and long-term scenarios for Mikey. By the end of the day, Jess's yawns were as wide and as long as Tom's. Again she went back to the shelter to help out and really enjoyed her time with the children.

Afterwards, Tom walked her out to her car and kissed her with repressed passion. They both needed to take things slowly, and at the moment that was just fine with Jess. Trust was a big issue for them both to overcome yet today Tom had opened up to her. He'd shared his feelings with the openness she'd come to expect.

'So why don't you just tell him about your family?' she

said out loud as she lay in bed that night. He'd been desperate to help Mikey and after his own upbringing he knew at first hand that not all families worked out. Jess sat up in bed as dawning realisation washed over her.

'That's it. Tom thinks I'm not *working* on the relationship with my family.' How was he supposed to know what Linda and her parents were really like? *She* hadn't told him. He'd only seen her reaction whenever her family called her. Jess saw her family's interference in her life as a hypocritical imposition. Tom probably saw it as a missed opportunity at reconciliation.

She lay back down and stared at the ceiling. So what was she going to do? What was the best way for Tom to experience what her family was like? He'd have to meet them, she rationalised, but shook her head. Every man Jess had been interested in had fallen victim to Linda's charms. There was no way she was going to risk losing Tom. She loved him. She hadn't loved any of the others. Did she trust Tom? Trust him enough to take him home and introduce him to Linda? Perhaps he might be immune to her sister.

Jess tossed and turned, knowing the answer was right in front of her but unsure whether she should take the chance. Finally, knowing she wouldn't get any sleep until she reached a decision, Jess decided to call her mother in the morning and accept the invitation to the Hamptons' party.

By Saturday, Jess still hadn't called her mother. Tom called around to help her transport her boxes to her new apartment. It was a small townhouse situated between the hospital and the shelter.

'So you're moving even closer to me now?' Tom joked as he helped her unpack. 'I can't believe how much stuff you don't have. How do you live like this?'

Jess shrugged. 'I get by.' Tom bought them lunch and afterwards they practised their balloon animals as they had another Clown Patrol coming up.

'This is really sad,' Tom said over the squeaky noise of the balloons.

'What?'

'We're both over thirty and look what we're doing!'

'Back up to the, "we're both over thirty" part'. She laughed and slugged him with a balloon. 'I'm not thirty for another four months.'

'Really? Are you going to have a party?'

'I doubt it. The last time I had a birthday party was...' Jess stared unseeingly at the balloon in her hands. 'Was five months before Scotty died.' The jovial atmosphere they'd been enjoying disappeared.

'What was he like?' The question was asked softly as Tom came over and sat beside her. They both leaned against the wall.

Jess smiled. 'He was wonderful. He never complained. Always had a smile on his face.'

'Was he well looked after?'

'Oh, yes. Nothing but the best of care for the politician's son.' Her tone was filled with pompous arrogance.

'And your parents? How did they cope with a disabled child?'

This was it, Jess thought. It was time for her to open up to Tom. Inside, a war was raging but she was slowly and surely beating it. She was quiet for such a long time that she thought Tom might get up and walk out. Indeed, when he did finally move she thought he was going to do just that and was about to beg him not to leave when she realised he was shifting.

'I know it's hard, Jessica,' he said as he faced her. He kissed her mouth and looked down into her eyes. 'Please, tell me.'

'When Scott was born my father crowed with joy, showering his son and heir with everything the boy desired. Yet when Scott was diagnosed with muscular dystrophy, he...rejected him.' She shook her head. 'My mother at least acknowledged the fact that she had a son and came to see him, but my father…' Jess looked down at her hands and realised she was trembling. She clenched them tighter and returned her gaze to Tom's. 'He said that from the very moment Scott was diagnosed, as far as he was concerned, his son had died.

'In some ways, I think I might have been able to accept that but, no, my father had to take it one step further. He realised that having a disabled son might help his political career. He campaigned for disability rights, which is a good thing but it was the way he did it. He cashed in on Scott's life, all the while completely ignoring him.'

Tom sucked in his breath in disgust.

'After Scott's funeral, which only I and the medical staff who'd looked after him attended, I moved out as soon as I could.' Jess clamped her jaws together, trying to control the tears that were threatening to spill over. 'My father wanted to have this big public funeral as he was due to run for re-election, but I put my foot down. As far as I was concerned, the farce was over. I blackmailed him, threatening to reveal the real truth about Hank Yeoman to the public. He knew I was serious.' Jess's voice broke on the last word and the tears began to trickle down her cheeks.

Tenderly, Tom wiped them away. 'Tell me more about Scott.'

Jess smiled immediately. 'He was gorgeous. He had a mop of brown curls and brown eyes. Just gorgeous. He had the sweetest, most giving and loving nature. I've never met anyone like him and I'm so honoured that he was my baby brother.

'I'd spend as much time with him as my studies would allow but I made sure that once a day, at least, I'd catch up with him. I was firmly entrenched in med school and whenever I'd had a stressful day, it was Scotty who would make me laugh.' She smiled for an instant but it soon faded. 'I miss him.' The tears started to flow again. 'Not once,

Tom. Not once did Scott ever speak of our father's rejection.' Jess hiccuped but continued, 'He would look at our father with those big brown eyes of his, hoping that one day he might gain our father's approval. He agreed to every public appearance, even when he wasn't doing too well.'

Without saying a word, Tom enveloped her in his arms, resting her head against his shoulder. 'He was gorgeous, Tom,' she said between sobs. 'So gorgeous. I loved him so much.'

The flood gates opened and Jess continued to cry as though her heart was breaking. Tom held her tightly, sometimes stroking her hair and murmuring soothing words. After about five minutes, the sobs started to subside.

'You've never shared your feelings with anyone, have you?'

Jess shook her head.

'Thank you,' he whispered, and pulled back to look at her. He smiled and tenderly wiped her eyes. 'Thank you, Jessica.'

'I probably look awful,' she said with a watery smile.

'Yeah.' He nodded slightly and it made her laugh. It made her love his honesty. It made her love *him* all the more. 'Come here.' He brought his mouth down to meet hers in a healing kiss. It said that he felt her pain and empathised with her. Jess gave herself up to his kisses.

Finally, Tom raised his head and looked at her. 'I think it's time you had a little rest,' he said in his best doctor voice. 'You're on duty tonight and, believe me, your boss won't be at all happy if you call in sick because you have the beginnings of a migraine.' Tom helped her to her feet and ushered her into the bedroom.

Jess laid down on top of the covers and watched as Tom knelt beside her. His knees cracked and she laughed. 'You old thing, you,' she teased. 'Tom?' she said a moment later after he'd taken her hand in his.

'Hmm?'

'Will you just…hold me?'

Tom smiled down into her face and brushed her hair out of her eyes. 'Of course.' He scrambled onto the futon, more bones creaking as he moved, causing Jess to laugh again.

'I don't think my bed agrees with you,' she said with a chuckle as he slid his arms around her. She breathed in deeply, allowing her lungs to be filled with the scent of his aftershave. He was warm and cosy. He was Tom. The man she loved.

'Feeling better?' he asked after a few minutes.

'Mmm.' Jess turned her face up to his, waiting to have her lips captured in one of his magnificent kisses. He didn't disappoint her.

'You're very special to me, Jessica,' he murmured as he kissed her eyes closed. 'Very special.' He kissed her forehead and her nose. 'You're like no other woman I've ever dated.' Tom nuzzled her neck and nipped at her ear lobe. Jess shivered in anticipation. 'Cold?' he asked, and when Jess opened her mouth to reply, she found her voice refused to work. Instead, she shook her head. 'Good.' Tom gathered her closer, their denim-clad legs intertwined.

'Your hair smells gorgeous,' he groaned, and placed a kiss on top of her head. 'Honestly, Jessica, when I'm with you, I feel as though everything is right with the world. It's such a strange sensation. One I've never felt before.'

Jess pulled back and gazed into his blue eyes. 'I know what you mean. It's…scary.'

'Taking the risk to trust someone with your feelings,' he stated, knowing exactly what she meant. Tom pressed his lips to hers, gently coaxing them apart.

She felt wonderful. Being in his arms, hearing him say how special she was. No one had ever uttered such charming and reassuring words to her before. It helped her to take that step—to try trusting Tom with her fragile heart. After all, what was love without trust?

The beat of her heart tattooed a rhythm against her ribs

that she was becoming familiar with. She was filled with such wonderment and delight that the sound reverberated through her ears as his kisses became more intense.

Jess didn't pull away. Instead, she threaded her fingers through his hair, ensuring he wasn't going to stop the sweet torture any time soon. She loved him so wholly and completely she thought she might burst. Tom was everything she'd ever wanted in a man and here she was, being held lovingly in his arms. What more could she ever want?

Tom eased back slightly, his breathing rapid, matching her own. She *was* special. They weren't just idle words he was muttering. For the first time in his life, he really meant it.

He slid his hand along her waist then brought it up, his thumb gently brushing the underside of her breast. Physically she was perfect and for a moment he wondered whether she was wearing those cute pink bunnies again or something else!

He watched as her eyelids fluttered closed at the contact, her breath catching in her throat. It was almost his undoing. To know that he affected her in such a way was a powerful aphrodisiac. He needed to remain in control. Jessica was too special to be rushed. Tom moved his hand up to her neck, the palm of his hand cupping her face.

She opened her eyes and gazed at him, the green depths filled with wanting. He moved his thumb, rubbing it lightly across her swollen lips.

Jess couldn't stop the explosion of desire that ripped through her at the slight contact. She parted her lips, her breathing heavy. Next, she kissed his thumb, drawing it into her mouth, gently sucking on it. Tom groaned and she relished the sound.

Moments later, he groaned again and, after moving his hand around to the back of her neck, Tom urged her mouth to meet his. This kiss wasn't sweet and gentle like the last time their lips had met. This one was hungry and searching.

A wave of delight washed over Jess as she leaned in closer to him, her breasts squashed against his chest.

She opened her mouth wider, returning his kisses with ardent passion. Higher and higher they rose, spiralling out of control. Tom brought his hand down, brushing her breast lightly again, causing Jess to catch her breath. At her back, Tom gently tugged her shirt from the waistband of her jeans and when his warm hand made contact with her skin, Jess broke her mouth from his as she gasped with pleasure.

She tipped her head back as she continued to suck air into her lungs. In some ways she felt as though she were drowning, and when Tom spread butterfly kisses across her neck she realised she was. Drowning with love for him.

Her skin was smooth yet hot to his touch. Tom caressed her back as she arched towards him. Through the sweet torture, Tom felt an anxiousness grip his heart. Jessica was more than special, she'd somehow become vitally important to his life. With surprise, he realised that his happiness didn't lie solely with himself any more.

He would never do anything to hurt her and although he wanted nothing more than to pursue this attraction further he realised that right now wasn't the time. They still had a lot of issues to work through. She'd been emotionally upset when they'd come into her room and Tom *never* wanted her to say he'd taken advantage of her.

'Tom,' she breathed, and moved her head so their lips could meet once again. His lips weren't as passionate as before and she realised he was withdrawing. Had she done something wrong? Had she disappointed him in some way? She was so new to this. Jess suddenly felt very out of her depth.

'Tom?' This time his name was a question. He shifted onto his back and urged her closer. She rested her head on his chest, listening to his heartbeat.

'Ah-h…Jessica. You feel so perfect in my arms.'

His words helped to comfort her a little but still she had unanswered questions.

'Did I do something wrong?' Her voice was shaking slightly and she didn't like feeling this vulnerable.

'What? No. Oh, honey, no.' Tom kissed her head.

'But you stopped.'

'Yes, I stopped.' He took a deep breath and slowly exhaled. 'You were upset about Scott and I don't want you to think I'd take advantage of you.'

'But I don't. Tom, I think we—'

'Shh,' he interrupted, and stroked her hair. 'You're too important to me, Jessica. I don't ever want to hurt you. Never intentionally.'

Jess closed her eyes and snuggled closer contentedly. The next time she opened her eyes, it was to find that the room had been plunged into darkness. She felt something heavy across her waist and realised it was Tom's arm. She now had her back to him and she snuggled in closer as she closed her eyes once more.

Her brain, however, refused to go back to sleep. Something was wrong.

She opened her eyes and glanced around the room. Yes, these were all her things but the room was different. That's right, she recalled. She'd moved apartments. On Saturday. Today was Saturday! 'Oh, no,' Jess gasped, and scrambled off the futon. The green digital clock display by her bed read that she had less than ten minutes to get to the hospital or she'd be late.

'Jessica?' Tom's sleepy voice made her turn in his direction. He slowly sat up and peered around the room for her.

'We fell asleep,' she told him as she quickly picked out a change of clothes and raced to the bathroom.

She heard him groaning and smiled to herself as she realised he was getting up from the futon. 'Coffee?' he asked from the other side of the door.

'No time.'

'You know, if you're late,' he called, his tone fading slightly as he walked away, 'I'll be forced to report you to your boss.'

Jess finished dressing and pulled the bathroom door open. 'Funny!' she called as she heard him fill the kettle. 'You don't have time for a coffee either,' she told him. 'At least, not here.' She pulled a brush through her hair while she dug out her shoes and slipped them on. Next, she loosely tied her hair back with a ribbon to keep it out of the way.

'I know. I'm getting it ready for when you return, bleary-eyed, just after six o'clock tomorrow morning.'

'How sweet. Come on. Get your stuff. We've got to go.' Jess grabbed her coat and bag and opened the door, waiting impatiently whilst Tom gathered up his own coat and keys.

'And that's it,' he joked as they walked out the door. 'I help her move, give her a kiss and a cuddle and then she throws me out.'

Jess smiled as she headed over to her car. 'Can't be helped.'

'Aren't you forgetting something?' he asked and she quickly retraced her steps. She kissed him three quick times on the lips and returned to the driver's side of the Jag. 'I can see we're going to have to work on your goodbyes,' he chided with a smile.

'See you tomorrow,' she called, before shutting her door and bringing the engine to life. She arrived at the hospital a whole five minutes late as she'd managed to get every single red light between her new apartment and the hospital. 'Always the way,' she grumbled as she put her things in her locker and went to find her colleague so he could hand over.

For a Saturday night in a children's hospital, A and E was fairly quiet. There was the usual rush around three a.m., with mothers bringing sick children in because of high temperatures and bad colds, but nothing too demanding.

Just after her shift finished, she went to the ward to check on Mikey. 'How's he doing?' she asked Joan, the ward clinical nurse consultant.

'Picking up. Poor kid didn't have a good night but Jack's more worried about the psychological injuries than the physical injuries.'

'Jack Holden—Kathryn's husband, right?' Jess questioned.

'That's right.' Joan smiled. 'It takes a while to get everyone straight.'

'I'm getting better,' Jess said.

'Well, you've obviously knocked our beloved Director of A and E for a six,' Joan commented.

Jess didn't reply. Instead, she simply shrugged her shoulders.

'Now you've embarrassed her,' a deep voice said from behind her, and Jess pivoted to see a man as tall as Tom smiling down at her. 'I'm Jack Holden,' he replied, and shook her hand.

'It's nice to meet you at last. I've read a lot of your articles on paediatric neurosurgery,' she said. 'I understand Mikey didn't have a very peaceful night?' Jess smothered a yawn as Jack pulled out Mikey's notes. Joan headed off to get ready for ward round.

'No. He woke up screaming on two separate occasions and was bathed in sweat. He's done that every night he's been here. I'm glad we were able to get him into a private room as this way he didn't wake too many of the other patients.'

'I know Tom wants to get him into a good foster-home sooner rather than later. Do you know how that's coming along?'

'Yes. Both Tom and I have a few meetings scheduled

later this morning with the ward social worker and the welfare department.'

'If you're meeting on a Sunday, it must be pretty urgent.'

'It is.'

'Tom told me the police report from the other day said they found definite proof that Mikey's dad did this to him.'

'That's right. Therefore, he'll be charged. As this isn't the first instance of something like this happening, it means Welfare can definitely step in.'

'It must be so nerve-racking. Poor Mikey.'

'You can say that again. Tom's already been on the phone this morning, making sure none of the meetings have been cancelled. He should be here any minute.'

Jess nodded, feeling suddenly revived at the prospect of seeing Tom.

'Busy night?' Jack asked.

'Not really, just long.'

'Do you want to see Mikey?'

'No. Let him rest.' When Jess yawned, they both laughed.

'Are you chatting up my girlfriend?' Tom said from the ward doorway, and they turned to look at him.

'On the contrary,' Jack replied as he shook hands with his friend. 'We were merely discussing a patient.'

'Just as well,' Tom said as he placed his arm about her waist and gave her a little squeeze. 'How was your night?'

'Fine, once I arrived.'

Tom smiled and Jess felt its full force as it warmed her right down to the tips of her toes. He was handsome in his suit but had looked even more gorgeous in his denim jeans yesterday.

He looked at Jack. 'Is there time for a cup of coffee before the meetings begin?'

'Sure. I'll do a quick ward round and meet you in the cafeteria,' he said with a grin. 'Go and say good morning to her properly!'

Tom laughed and Jess merely smiled. 'It was nice to finally meet you, Jack.'

'Likewise,' he said. 'Kathryn and I will have to arrange a time when we can have the two of you over.'

Tom nodded. 'Sounds good.' He reached for Jess's hand. 'Now…for some coffee.' They headed to the cafeteria with Jess unsuccessfully smothering a few yawns. 'I thought our little impromptu nap might have taken the edge off your tiredness,' he said softly by her ear.

'It did. It got me through the night. Right now, my body's saying it's time for a longer sleep.'

'You can just tell your gorgeous body that it's also time for a cup of coffee with the man who finds it hard to take his eyes off you.'

'Well…when you put it like that…' She laughed, allowing him to steer her to a table. Once she was seated, he poured them both a coffee and brought them over. They discussed what had happened during her shift and Tom's upcoming meetings with the social worker and Welfare.

When they'd finished their drinks, Jess took Tom's hand in hers and looked across the table at him. 'Tom. There's something I'd like to discuss with you.'

'Is everything all right?' He was instantly alert.

'Sort of. It has to do with my family.'

Tom relaxed a little but held firmly to her hand.

Jess took a deep breath, trying to find the words to calmly tell him what was going on in her life. 'My mother and sister have been calling me more in the past few weeks for a reason.'

'Why?'

'Both of them keep asking me to go to Cairns for a party.'

'A party?'

'Yes. A family called the Hamptons are having a big socialite party this coming weekend and my sister and mother have been trying to persuade me to attend.' Jess looked down at their entwined hands. 'My father has even offered to pay for my air ticket.'

'Is that a good thing?'

'Put it this way, I don't trust this idea for that reason alone. My father hasn't spoken to me since I left his house seven years ago.'

'So the fact that he's going to pay for your ticket makes you suspicious.'

'Yes. Look, perhaps this isn't the right time to discuss it,' she said as she yawned. 'I just wanted to let you know that I was thinking of going.'

'So you want the weekend off?'

'Well, if I decide to go. The thing is, I'm not sure if it's the right thing to do. I feel as though I'm walking into a trap.'

'Then again, their motives might be real. Your father might be ready to make amends.'

'Perhaps…but if that's the case, why would they invite me home *just* for this party? Why not ask me to simply come home?'

'Good point. Do you know anything about this Hampton family?'

'Yes. Our families have been friends for years. According to Linda, Mr Hampton is now in a position to be of great benefit to my father's career.'

'What does your father do again?'

'He's in politics. He's planning to run for State Premier in the next election.'

'That's big-time playing.'

'Yes. Look, I wanted you to know so—'

'I could roster you off. Sure. If you need to go, then you need to go.'

'No, Tom. The reason I wanted you to know was that…' Jess stopped and took a deep breath. 'I want you to come, too. I want you to meet my family.'

CHAPTER NINE

TOM walked into his apartment and pulled off his tie. One meeting after the other was definitely wearing but he'd been determined to come up with a solution today. Thanks to one of his contacts, they'd managed to successfully place Mikey in a temporary foster-home. They needed to wait for the court hearing and for other bits of red tape to be cleared up before placing Mikey permanently. If Jack was satisfied with their patient's condition, Mikey would be leaving the hospital the following morning and hopefully starting a new life—away from his father.

It made him reflect on how his life might have been made worse had his parents chosen to live. 'No use wondering about what-ifs,' he mumbled as he filled the kettle. His thoughts turned to Jessica and her request that he accompany her back to Cairns. She *wanted* him to meet her family. Surely that was a good sign.

His phone shrilled to life and he quickly picked up the cordless phone and returned to the kitchen. 'Dr Bryant.'

'How did things go with Mikey?' Nicola asked.

'Good.' Tom leaned against the bench.

'That's it? Good?'

'Yes.'

'Something else has happened. What's going on, Tommy?'

'No pulling the wool over your eyes, is there?' He smiled. 'Jessica asked me to accompany her to Cairns this weekend.'

'Why?'

'To meet her family.'

'Wow!' He could tell that Nicola was just as impressed

as he had been. 'So it's serious between the two of you, then?'

'She's…well, she's amazing, Nicola. I'm glad she's opening up and talking about her family.'

'Have you told her about your childhood?'

'Some of it.'

'Ooh, this really sounds serious.'

'You know how difficult it is for me to open up—especially to a woman—but Jessica…she's so different.'

'It's probably because she hasn't had it easy herself,' Nicola surmised. 'Do you know much about her family?'

'Not really.'

'Are you going with her?'

'I'm not sure. It depends if I can change the rosters in time.'

'Do you want to go?'

'I'll admit I'm curious about her family and I want to be there to support her. She's almost positive it's some sort of trap that her parents are setting in asking her to go home, and from things she's told me about them they don't sound too…trustworthy.'

'Case closed, then.' Nicola said.

'Meaning?' The kettle boiled and switched itself off Tom didn't move, too engrossed with what his surrogate sister was saying.

'You've already decided to go. Support Jessica because that may be all she really needs from you. Think about it. When we were fostered by Merle and Alwyn, what was the one difference with them as opposed to all the other families we were with?'

'Support.'

'Exactly. Jessica doesn't necessarily *need* you to meet her family. She needs you there to support *her* when she meets them again.'

Tom knew what he had to do. 'I'll change the rosters first thing in the morning.'

The next day he did just that and paged Jessica to let her know. She thanked him politely but didn't say anything more. As the week progressed, Tom noticed that she started withdrawing further and further into herself and he didn't blame her.

By the time Nicola and her family waved them off at the airport on Saturday morning, Jess was a nervous wreck. 'I shouldn't be going,' she told him as their plane taxied along the runway.

Tom took her hand in his and kissed it. 'You'll be fine.' They'd flown business class, giving them a bit more room as well as a bit more privacy.

'This was a mistake,' Jess said when they were on the last leg of their journey. She turned wild eyes to stare at him. 'I can't see them, Tom.'

'Jessica.' He placed his arm about her shoulders and held her. 'Everything will be all right. I'm here for you.'

'I know, but you don't know them. They're not nice people, Tom.'

'Shh,' he soothed. 'They're expecting us now, so let's just go and see what unfolds.'

Jess raised her head and shook it.

'What?' he asked gently.

'They're not expecting *us,* they're expecting *me.*'

Tom was silent for a whole two seconds. 'You didn't tell them I was coming with you?'

'No.'

'Why not?'

'Because I know they have something…*planned* and, well, by bringing you along it helps give me an edge. My element of surprise.'

'Do you have some sort of inkling as to what might happen?'

Jess rested her head back against the seat but continued to hold his hand. 'I'm not sure.' She closed her eyes and sighed. 'I've been racking my brain all week long, trying to figure out what's going on. What might happen. How I'll react. I just don't know. All I do know is that I don't trust my father. He won't be completely happy until he's running my life again.' Jess opened her eyes and gazed at him. 'I didn't want to tell them I was bringing you because I didn't want to give them time to react.'

'Catch them by surprise.'

'Well, yes.'

'So you're using me,' Tom stated.

'No!' Jess was horrified he should think such a thing. 'Tom, how could you even think that? I want you with me because I…I derive strength from you. You…you help me keep things in perspective and because I…' Jess stopped. She'd almost said it. She held her breath.

'Because what?' Tom's gaze didn't waver from her own. Jess's breath whooshed out of her lungs and under his intense gaze she felt her heart rate increase. Her stomach lurched as the plane lost altitude, getting ready to land.

'Because…' She swallowed, her mouth suddenly dry. She took a deep breath and met his gaze. This was it. The moment of truth. 'Because I love you, Tom,' she whispered. Tears started to gather in her eyes and she bit her lower lip. 'I didn't mean to fall in love with you but…' she shrugged '…I have.'

Tom enveloped her in his arms as the wheels of the plane touched the runway. He held her until the plane had stopped and it was time for them to disembark. He kissed her lips but didn't say anything about her declaration. It left Jess feeling even more vulnerable than before.

'Jessie,' Linda crooned as they walked into the terminal. Tom watched as the tall, immaculate blonde rushed over to Jessica's side. She kissed the air on either side of her sister's cheeks before turning and staring blatantly at Tom.

'Ooh,' she sang as her gaze devoured Tom like a child who's just unwrapped a new toy. 'Is this one yours?' Linda came around to Tom's other side and threaded her arm through his. 'My sister and I share *everything*,' Linda purred, and Jess felt sick. 'Why don't you go and get the bags, Jessie, while handsome and I become...better acquainted?'

Jess worked very hard at holding onto her temper. 'We've only brought hand luggage,' she informed her sister between clenched teeth.

'Well, then, the car's waiting outside.' She smiled seductively at Tom. 'Shall we?'

They walked out to the car, Tom between the two sisters. He marvelled at how completely different they were and was beginning to understand some of Jessica's earlier reluctance to return home.

The stretch limousine had plenty of room for them to be seated quite comfortably yet when Linda decided to sit on top of him he almost choked on her perfume.

'So...aren't you going to tell me your name?' she whispered, touching his ear with her perfectly manicured fingernail. 'I don't bite—well, only when it's warranted.' She arched her neck and laughed, and Tom almost joined her—but not for the same reasons. She was...ludicrous.

'Tom. My name is Tom.'

'Tom,' she drawled, and licked her lips.

Deciding he'd had enough, he shifted slightly and put his bag on the seat next to him, hopefully giving Jessica's pushy sister the message.

Jess, on the other hand, found it hard to look at Tom— especially after her declaration of love. She looked out of the tinted window at the beautiful sunny day. It wasn't hot, not by any stretch of the imagination, as it was only August, but Cairns was still nice and sunny, even during winter. Why wasn't it raining and stormy? She growled at the weather, cross that it didn't reflect her mood.

She risked a glance at Tom and found him watching her. No doubt he was trying to decide how she compared to the stunningly beautiful Linda. Perhaps he was wondering why he'd even pursued her. Jess's insecurities started to raise their ugly heads and she recalled it was just another reason why she'd stayed away from her family since Scott's death. They had the ability to bring her down faster than any rainstorm. They'd have all her previous neuroses up and intact within a few hours—if she let them.

Tom watched Jessica become more and more agitated. She fiddled with the zipper on her bag, flicked her nails and ran her fingers through her hair over a dozen times. She'd said she derived strength from him so as they drove through a set of large, wrought-iron gates and up the sweeping driveway Tom decided on his course of action.

As soon as the car stopped, someone came to open the door. Tom waited for Linda to climb out before quickly coming and sitting beside Jessica. He gathered her into his arms and kissed her. 'Whatever you need me for, Jessica, I'm here,' he told her softly. 'You're very special to me. Understand?'

Jess clung to him for a moment longer before pulling back suddenly. Plain speaking had always been paramount between them and she decided that now, especially, shouldn't be any different. 'Do you fancy Linda?'

'What?' Tom gave her an incredulous look. 'No. No! No way! Is that what's been bothering you? That she'll try and take me away like your other boyfriends?' When Jess nodded, Tom crushed her to him again. 'Oh, Jessica. No. Honey, *you're* my type. Remember?' He kissed her and Jess started to feel better. She breathed in, drawing strength from him.

'We've got to be completely honest with each other during our time here,' she whispered as she heard Linda's footsteps returning to the car, obviously wondering what was keeping them. 'There are so many lies in this house that honesty is the only way we'll survive.'

'Agreed,' he said, and pressed his lips to hers, knowing full well that Linda would witness it. Good, he thought.

The sooner her family knew that Jessica belonged to him, the better. Even as the thought crossed his mind, Tom realised that he believed it. His feelings for Jessica were so...powerful, especially after she'd declared her love for him.

'Oh!' Linda remarked as she poked her head back through the limo door. 'That's why you were taking so long. Hurry up. Mummy and Daddy are waiting, Jessie.'

As they climbed out of the car, Tom held Jess's hand firmly. He knew she didn't like being called Jessie and he could understand why. The way her sister said the name made her sound like an insignificant servant, instead of the first-born child.

Jess didn't recognise any of the servants but that wasn't anything new. Her father usually took to firing people when they made mistakes. They followed the butler into the sitting-room where her mother was sitting, her back ram-rod straight, doing some embroidery. Jess felt as though they'd stepped back a century or two. Only her mother's stylish suit testified to the change in era.

'Oh, my word, Jessie,' her mother said as she stood, glaring pointedly at Tom and the way he held her daughter's hand. 'You've...brought a little friend with you. Really, dear,' her mother said as she kissed the air on either side of Jess's cheek. 'You should have warned me.'

'I didn't think it would be any bother,' Jess said, feeling more like herself again. 'There are certainly more than enough guest rooms.'

'Of course. So, who is this...handsome man you've brought with you?'

'Mummy,' Linda chimed in as she once again took Tom's free arm in hers. 'I'd like you to meet...Tom.'

'Tom? Tom who?'

'Tom Bryant,' he answered. 'I work with Jessica.'

'Oh! You're a doctor, then. Well, well. Bryant? Bryant?'

Mrs Yeoman tossed the name around thoughtfully. 'Are your parents the Bryants who live in Spain?'

'No.' Tom didn't feel the need to justify himself to Jessica's mother, and as she seemed intent on putting him down he didn't feel guilty about it. He felt Jessica squeeze his hand and knew they had to get out of there. 'It's been a long flight. So if someone could show us to our *room*, we'd appreciate it,' he stated, and for a second Mrs Yeoman baulked.

'But of course,' she said, recovering beautifully. 'Fotherington will show you.' She rang a little bell. Moments later the butler reappeared and was given his instructions.

'Show Miss Jessie to her room—we've kept it for you, dear—and Dr Bryant will stay in the aubergine room.'

'Very good, ma'm,' he said with a small bow. Wow, they really had him well trained, Jess thought as she and Tom followed Fotherington.

'Actually, Fotherington,' Jess said as they proceeded up a staircase, 'I'll have the room next to the aubergine room.'

'Why?' Tom asked.

'Well, unless my mother has renamed every room in the house, which is highly possible, we'll be at opposite ends. You in one wing, me in another.'

'Trying to separate us, are they?'

'Apparently so.' It appeared that Fotherington was more fond of his job than Jess had surmised as he patiently showed Jess to her old bedroom. 'Wow,' she said as she walked in through the door. It looked exactly the same as it had for the past twenty-nine years. Little pink love-hearts lined the walls and the frilly, pink bedspread shouted out that this was a room any little girl would love. 'I'm amazed.'

'Very pretty.' Tom nodded.

'Yeah. If you're six! As a teenager I begged them to let me change it and once I even started tearing the wallpaper off the walls. When I returned home from school, it was back to normal as though nothing had happened.' She shook her head. 'Sorry. I'm not sleeping in here.'

'You can always share the aubergine room with me,' he said quietly, a mischievous gleam in his eyes.

'That's a brilliant idea.' Jess laughed and decided on impulse to do just that. Holding firmly to her bag, she asked Fotherington to show them to the aubergine room.

'Yes, Miss Jessie,' he said with a small bow.

'Why is it called the aubergine room? Are there egg-plants all around it?' Tom whispered as they walked down another long corridor.

'Wait and see,' she said, and when Fotherington opened the door it was to reveal a room filled with different shades of purple.

'Nice,' he said.

'Pre-dinner drinks will be in half an hour,' Fotherington stated, before leaving them.

Tom took Jessica's bag from her. 'Very nice,' he said as he walked around the room. 'It screams money.'

'Really? I thought it screamed, "let me out of here".'

Tom laughed, opening his arms to Jess. 'Thank you for asking me to come,' he whispered as he stroked her hair.

'I'm glad you came.'

'Together, we stand. Divided, we fall,' he misquoted, and pulled back to kiss her. 'Are you sure you're all right about sharing?'

Jess nodded. 'It's just for one night.'

'How about you go first in the shower?'

'Good idea. We don't want to keep them waiting.'

Tom watched her pick up her bag and head towards the *en suite*. She was happy again. His Jessica was happy again and, amazingly, she made him feel just as happy.

When Tom came out of the bathroom, Jess stared at him. He was dressed in a tuxedo and he looked…good enough to eat. 'Tom,' she gasped, drinking her fill of him. 'You are one handsome man.'

'You don't scrub up too bad yourself,' he said as he held her arms out to gaze at her. The bodice of her outfit was cream embroidered silk which she wore off the shoulder, revealing her soft, elegant neck. The skirt was full-flowing royal blue silk that reached her ankles. A matching blue stole was draped around her lower arms and her hair was loose, brushed back behind her ears. She wore only blue sapphire earrings and no necklace.

'It's only hired,' she said.

'You should buy it,' he murmured with a slow nod. 'It's looks perfect on you.' Tom groaned and gathered her to him, unable to resist the lure of her neck any longer. 'Jessica, you're stunning,' he breathed, and she closed her eyes, arching her head back a little. With the addition of her heels they were equal in height, which made it all the easier for Tom to find her lips and kiss her senseless.

Jess felt as though she was going to explode with love for him and held him firmly to her as her heart pounded with joy. When he pulled back, both of them breathing heavily, he gazed at her once more—a crooked smile on his lips.

'I think you may need to repair your lipstick,' he said.

'Well, I think you may need to brush your hair again,' she countered. They laughed and Tom took three huge steps away from her.

'If I don't put distance between us, we'll never make it downstairs.'

'Sounds like a better plan to me,' Jess replied as she headed back to the bathroom. Within a few minutes Tom shut the door to the aubergine room and, with Jessica's arm tucked firmly in the crook of his elbow, they headed down the corridor. 'Here goes nothing,' she murmured as they descended the stairs.

When they arrived in the drawing room for pre-dinner

drinks, Hank Yeoman greeted Tom with great interest. He was smooth—always the politician. They all travelled to the party in a stretch limousine where they were met by their hosts.

Half an hour later Jess watched as Tom politely made his way through the crowded ballroom, heading back towards her. 'I'm sure sheep aren't jammed in this tight,' he said when he finally reached her side.

'The less room there is to move, the more successful the party. At least, I think that's how it works.' She smiled at him but turned when someone tapped her on the shoulder.

'Jessie!' A tall blond man gathered her in his arms and pressed his mouth firmly to hers. 'You look fabulous.'

Tom's urge to protect Jess, not only from her family but from anyone else who threatened to destroy her world, magnified in that one instant. He clenched his jaw, his eyes blazing with anger as he glared at the intruder.

'S-Sean,' Jess stuttered in surprise, before glancing at Tom. Oh, no. She could tell he was angry and she didn't blame him. Sean had kissed her as though he was ready to scoop her up and carry her off to bed. She opened her mouth to speak, to introduce the two men before anything worse could happen.

'Let me look at you,' Sean said, and shifted his stance to better admire her figure. 'It must be at least seven or eight years since we've seen each other. You've changed. *A lot!*' His gaze swept over her again and Jess had to control the urge not to shudder.

'I'll thank you,' Tom said evenly, his gaze boring into Sean as though he'd like to rearrange the man's pretty face. 'not to speak to my girlfriend like that.' Tom secretly enjoyed the look of terror that crossed the other man's face, but as he went to place a protective arm about Jessica's shoulders he felt someone else grab his arm.

'Bryant,' Hank Yeoman said, his tone menacingly polite. 'Let's talk.'

Jess shook her head and reached for Tom but her father had already pulled him out of her grasp.

Tom shrugged free and took a step towards her, kissing her possessively. 'I won't be long,' he said, and turned to follow her father. Jess watched him go, her anxiety mounting with each step he took away from her. What was her father going to say? How would Tom react to her father's interference?

Her stomach lurched.

'Jessie?'

She turned to look at Sean.

'Jessie? You don't look at all well.'

She allowed Sean to lead her through the crowd, listening to him mumble about her needing some space. He led her out of the ballroom and down a corridor. She felt much better simply being out of the crowd.

'This should do,' he said as he opened a door. 'We can talk in here.' The walls were lined with books and there were comfortable leather chairs perfectly suitable for curling up in with a good book. He led her over to a chair and waited while she sat. He stared into her face and nodded. 'You're looking a bit better.'

He walked over to the ornamental mantelpiece. 'Jessie, I'm sorry. I had no idea you were dating someone. I would never have kissed you otherwise.' He paused and shook his head. 'I was led to believe you were interested in me. Well, you know, pursuing…something with me.'

Jess sighed heavily and leaned her head back against the chair, her eyes closing for a moment. 'Who told you?'

'My parents—both of them—as well as your father. They've been telling me for months how you've been wanting to see me again. To try dating again.'

'Sean, we've never dated.'

'I know but the…*intent* has always been there.'

'You mean that at the age of about two our parents decided that we should get married?'

'Our families have been friends for such a long time. I'll admit I wasn't overly attracted to you when you were younger, but I've watched the ugly duckling mature into a beautiful swan. You look stunning tonight.'

'What about Linda?'

Sean frowned. 'Linda? What does she have to do with this?'

Jess stood, feeling stronger than before. 'Linda has always been the beautiful swan. Remember the summer you came home from boarding school?'

'I came home most summers,' he pointed out.

'You know which one I'm talking about. I was fourteen. You were sixteen. Linda was thirteen and a lot more…physically developed than I was. You came home from boarding school for the summer.'

She watched as Sean hung his head for a moment before nodding. 'I remember.'

'You flirted with me. Kissed me. I thought it was the most romantic thing that had ever happened to me. Then the next day I found you kissing Linda.'

Sean shrugged. 'I was sixteen. My hormones were in overdrive. Don't tell me you've been holding a grudge all these years?'

Jess chuckled mirthlessly and rolled her eyes. 'No, Sean, but it was a turning point in my life. Up until then I'd thought it was only my father I couldn't trust. You showed me that the male species in general were untrustworthy.

'As the years went on and Linda found it necessary to intercept every other male I became interested in, my initial perceptions were confirmed. Now, I've met a man who has shown me that I *can* trust him. That he *does* support me. *Me*, Sean. The *real* me.

'My advice to you is to find out who *you* are. That way, when your parents start saying that a woman you haven't seen for seven years is interested in you, you'll be able to view the situation objectively and make up your own mind.'

'Jessie, I—'

'My name is Jess. See, you don't even know that I've hated that name—for years.'

'But your friend does?'

'Yes. Tom does. I love him, Sean, and no one—especially my father—is going to separate us.'

'You have such…inner strength,' he marvelled.

'It's always been there.'

'I just never took the time to find out.'

'Exactly.'

'What are you going to do now?'

'Now? I'm going to find Tom and try to explain this mess to him.' She should have told Tom about Sean before they'd come, she realised as Sean held the door open for her. Her father had probably spouted all sorts of rubbish to Tom, which she was determined to patiently wade through. There was no way in the world she was going to lose Tom.

They walked up the corridor and re-entered the noisy ballroom. Jess searched for Tom, her inner turmoil mounting with each passing second she failed to find him. She spotted her father talking to Mr Hampton so she knew that Tom was no longer with him. So where was he?

'Jessie, darling,' her mother crooned. 'Come and meet…'

Jess wasn't listening. She spotted Tom in a corner, talking earnestly to someone. Jess shifted, trying to see who it was that had captured his attention so completely.

'Jessie?' She felt her mother tugging on her arm. 'Please, Jessie. Come on.'

Just as she started to turn away, in her peripheral vision she saw someone put their arms about Tom's neck. Jess spun around, watching in horror as Tom smiled and hugged Linda close before her sister pressed her lips to Tom's.

'*No!*' Jess whispered in horror.

CHAPTER TEN

'JESSIE.' Mrs Yeoman's tone was firm and she tugged harder on her daughter's arm. Jess turned to glare at her mother as her world started to crumble. She felt ill. Mentally and physically ill. Not Tom. Not Tom! Her heart was screaming in pain as all her childhood neuroses came flooding back to swamp her.

She looked wildly at her mother and realised that she, too, had witnessed the kiss. 'It's for the best,' her mother hissed, her smile still in place.

'Jess?' She looked over her shoulder to see Sean. 'I'll take her, Mrs Yeoman,' he said politely, and started to steer her away. Thankfully, her mother released her. 'Jess, you look worse than before,' Sean murmured as he once again started to shift through the crowd. 'I saw it, too, Jess. It doesn't mean anything. I'm sure it's just another misunderstanding. Tonight seems to be filled with them.'

Jess felt her knees begin to buckle and Sean tightened his arm about her waist. 'Hold on, Jess. We're almost there.'

It was then that Jess realised Sean was taking her straight over to where Tom and Linda were standing. Tom was still smiling at her sister and Jess's heart lurched in pain.

A fine melodious sound of someone tapping a crystal glass filled the room. People stopped talking and turned their attention towards the small stage where the classical quartet had previously been playing. Mr Hampton stepped up to the microphone. 'Excuse me,' he said, still waiting for complete silence.

Jess glanced over at Tom again. They were about half

the room away from him and now that the noise had died down they couldn't move.

'Thank you all for coming,' Mr Hampton began, and started his speech. He spoke about her father and his many accomplishments. Then her father was invited up onto the stage where it was announced he'd be running for State Premier at the next election.

Her father thanked Mr Hampton for his continued support and then announced that he hoped to have everyone gather together within the next few months to celebrate another joyous event. 'But we don't want to embarrass Sean and Jessie too much, do we?' Hank chuckled. 'Only to say that it's about time our two families became united in a personal way.'

Everyone clapped and looked towards Sean and Jess. She was completely shocked. She'd thought her father was low but nothing like this! She glanced at Sean, to see that he reciprocated her feelings.

She looked over at Tom, only to find his head down. Tears started to well behind her eyes and she quickly turned away. Surely he didn't believe these lies? He knew her better than that. He knew she loved him. She'd told him as much.

Just then a loud cry pierced the noise and everyone turned to look. It was Linda. She was clutching her stomach in agony and looking very green. Jess watched as Tom eased her sister to the ground, speaking to her all the time. Jess moved towards her. All previous feelings of inadequacy disappeared as the professional inside her took over.

People stood back to let her through. When she reached Linda, it was to see that her skin was beaded with perspiration, her eyes wild with a mixture of fright and pain.

'Pulse is fast, breathing shallow,' Tom reported when Jess crouched down on the other side of her sister. 'Painful abdomen.'

'Appendix?' she queried.

'Possible. Gastroenteritis is another possibility.'

'Linda?' Jess called, and Linda groped for her sister's arm.

'Jessie? Jessie? What's happening?' she wailed in fright.

'It's all right, Linda. We're going to get you to hospital.' She glanced up at the crowd and realised that Sean had followed her. 'Call an ambulance,' she told him. 'And get these people away. She needs some room.'

'R-right,' Sean stuttered, but stood where he was, his face registering his shock.

'Move,' Tom ordered, and people quickly turned and did as he'd commanded. 'Jessica, try loosening those buttons at the back of her dress.'

'Right.' Jess did as he asked but the instant she tried to move Linda, her sister groaned in agony. 'Sorry, Linda. Your dress is too tight and the restriction might be causing extra strain.'

Linda clutched at her sister's arm again. 'Jessie. Don't let me die. Not like Scott. Don't let me die.'

'You're not going to die,' Jess told her sister firmly. 'What have you eaten?'

'Nothing. Felt too sick.'

Tom and Jess looked at each other. 'Has this happened before?' Jess asked.

'Yes. This is how Scott got sick. I have it, don't I? I have what he had. I've caught it,' Linda wailed and started to cry. Jess sighed and smoothed her sister's hair back from her forehead.

'You don't have what Scott had. You don't have muscular dystrophy, Linda.'

'How can you be sure?' Linda sobbed.

'Because I am, now shush,' Jess soothed. 'When we get you to the hospital, they'll run some tests.' Jess glanced at Tom. 'That ambulance could take for ever. Perhaps we should get her into a limo and take her to the hospital ourselves.'

'We'll give it a few more minutes,' he said.

One of the catering staff brought over a bowl of cool water and some towels, and Jess started to sponge her sister's forehead. 'Linda?' she asked. 'Did you take anything for the pain?'

'Some white tablets.'

'When?'

'Before we left to come here.'

'What were they?' Jess asked.

'I don't know.'

'Where did you get them from?' Tom asked.

'Pierre.'

'Who?' Tom looked at Jess.

'The cook.' She nodded. 'It was probably paracetamol. Pierre has been with our family since we were children. He looks on Linda as the daughter he never had.'

'Well, at least someone was looking out for her.'

'Ambulance is here,' someone behind them said, and Jess breathed a sigh of relief.

'Hear that? Time for you to go to hospital, Linda.'

'I don't want to go,' Linda protested, and started to cry again, but another round of pain started to rack her body and she cried out. Jess continued wiping her forehead and soon they had her transferred to the stretcher.

'You're going to be fine.'

'Don't leave me, Jessie,' her sister pleaded.

'I'm not going anywhere.' Regardless of how or why Linda had hurt Jess in the past, it had nothing to do with what was happening now. Their first priority was to get Linda diagnosed and stabilised—*then* Jess would start sorting things out.

They sat in the back of the ambulance, monitoring Linda's condition. 'It could be anything,' she said as they set up an IV. Tom administered something to relieve Linda's pain and it helped her to relax and doze a little.

The atmosphere in the confined space was stifling. They

both focused on Linda, checking her observations again. 'Do you know much about your sister's medical history?'

Jess thought for a moment. 'Tonsillectomy when she was four.' She shrugged. 'After that, I really don't remember.'

'But you remember when she had her tonsils out,' he stated.

'Yes.' Jess smiled into the distance and shook her head slightly. 'I remember Pierre giving her this little gold bell and telling her to ring it any time she needed something. She rang that damn thing constantly.'

'How old were you?'

'I was five. Her room was near mine so I found it was quite a noisy time. When I complained to Pierre, he told me I was always whining about one thing or another and couldn't I see that his precious little Linda was sick.'

Tom nodded but didn't say anything else. Jess felt as though he was slipping away from her. Maybe things *wouldn't* work out. Maybe there had been too much damage done tonight to salvage the wonderful relationship they'd built up. It had been a huge mistake to bring Tom home to meet her family and one she'd regret for ever.

The paramedics announced their arrival at the hospital and within seconds the ambulance was brought to a halt.

As Linda was wheeled inside, the paramedics gave a handover to the staff and Tom told them about the pain relief before he and Jess were shown to the family waiting room.

'I've never been in a family waiting room before,' Tom murmured as he looked at the decor. 'Well, not as a family member,' he clarified. Inside, he was still seething with rage because of what Jess's father had told him. When was going to be the right time to confront Jess. Why hadn't she trusted him?

A member of staff came to tell them that Linda had appendicitis and would be taken to surgery immediately.

'She'll be fine,' Tom said to Jess. Even though his words were nice, his tone was still brisk.

'I know. I just wonder how long she's had the symptoms and not said anything. Poor Linda.' Jess shook her head sadly as she sat down. 'Thinking she was contracting muscular dystrophy. It must have scared her half out of her mind.'

'Did she ever try to tell you about the pain?' he asked.

Jess frowned. 'Not that I can recall.'

'How often would she call you?' His tone was accusatory as he started to pace up and down the small room.

'Two or three times a week.'

'And she never once said she was having abdominal pain.'

'No.'

'And what? You didn't bother to ask her how she was? In general?'

'Why are you mad at me?'

'Because you're her sister, Jessica. I've seen how your parents treat both of you. You were the only one she could turn to.'

'You know nothing about my relationship or my phone calls with Linda.'

'And why is that, do you suppose?' he questioned, his tone laced with irony. 'Probably because you haven't trusted me enough to tell me about them. You say you love me but love is nothing without trust, Jessica.'

'After tonight's little performance of you kissing Linda, I think I've been very wise not to trust you.'

'So you admit it! You admit that you don't trust me?'

Jess was silent. How had things gone so terribly wrong in such a short space of time? She watched him pace around the room, stopping every now and then to look at her. It was the look of a stranger.

'I guess,' he continued, 'that's why you didn't bother to tell me about Sean Hampton.'

Jess floundered, knowing he had her there. 'I should have.'

'You're darned right you should have. Imagine my surprise when your father takes me aside and tells me that you and Sean have been…how did he put it…intended for each other for years.'

'You can't believe—'

'I'm not saying I believe what he said, Jessica. An arranged marriage is an outdated, ludicrous idea that never would have worked. I know you, remember. Or at least I thought I did. What I'm amazed at is that you forgot to mention this little fact to me before we arrived.

'I asked you if you knew who the Hamptons were yet you forgot to mention that your father had hopes of marrying you off with their oldest son. To top it all off, I then find this Sean bloke ogling my girlfriend right before my eyes.'

'You have every right to be cross.'

'You're darned right I do. Open and honest, Jessica. You were the one who said we needed to remain open and honest with each other. I don't care about your father's deceptions, they're meaningless. What I *do* care about is that you kept this from me. You lied.'

'Oh, and you didn't?' How dared he make out that she was the only person in the wrong here. He'd been kissing her sister!

'What's that supposed to mean?'

Jess clenched her teeth. 'You told me Linda wasn't your type, and I believed you.'

It was Tom's turn to frown. 'She isn't my type.'

'Then why were you kissing her earlier tonight?' Tom had the decency to pale as she spoke. 'Yes, I saw it,' she told him. 'So don't try to deny it.' Jess stood and turned her back to him. Hot tears stung in her eyes and she blinked them away. 'Linda has had everything,' she told him. 'All of her life she's been favoured. Do you have any idea how

that felt?' She turned to look at him again. 'I've been pe-
nalized by my parents simply because I wasn't as beautiful
as Linda. It's taken me *years* to work through my confused
emotions. Admittedly, Scott helped, but we were like two
peas in a pod. Neither of us were good enough to win
approval from our parents.' Tears spilled over onto her
cheeks and she impatiently brushed them away. 'Linda was
the ''golden child''. She's had everything, Tom, and now
she's set her sights on you.' Jess's voice broke on a sob.
'I knew I shouldn't have come home.'

'You're right, Jessica. She's had everything, except her
sister's respect.'

'Huh. Respect! Linda doesn't know what the word
means. She sees something she wants and she takes it.'

'You're wrong.'

'I beg your pardon. I suppose you're the expert on my
sister after sharing a few kisses with her.' The tears were
coming hard and fast now and Jess was powerless to stop
them. 'Do we compare? Is she better?' Jess couldn't go on.
She closed her eyes and hung her head. The man she loved,
the man she'd thought she could trust, had deceived her.

She flinched as Tom's arms came about her but he was
too strong for her to break free. 'Don't!' she sobbed. 'Don't
touch me.' She balled her hands into fists and feebly hit at
his chest.

'Shh,' he soothed as he continued to hold her. 'Shh. This
was the wrong time, honey.' He felt awful. He should have
realised that she was so taut with emotions that now hadn't
been the right time to discuss things. Still, one thing had
led to another and he hadn't been able to stop it. Now she
was so upset she could hardly drag enough air into her
lungs to support her sobs.

'She's not my type. *You're* my type. Shh, honey. It'll be
all right. We'll work things through.' He held her, murmuring soothing words until her sobs subsided. Tom led
her over to the chair and sat down, his arm still around her.

'I saw you, Tom,' she whispered. 'I saw you kissing Linda.'

'No. You saw Linda kissing me, and it wasn't for the reasons you're thinking.'

'But—'

'Are you going to let me explain or not?'

Jess nodded.

'Linda did try coming on to me again after I'd had a chat with your father. I held her at arm's length and told her that, regardless of the plans your father had, I had different ones. They included you and I being together for the rest of our lives.'

Jess gasped at his words, her green eyes wide with surprise.

'I wasn't going to let you go without a fight. It was then that Linda told me that your father had ordered her to break us up. She'd stolen so many of your boyfriends in the past that he knew it was a thorn in your side. She also told me that she was interested in Sean Hampton and wasn't too happy with the way your father was manipulating the situation.'

'You're joking!' Jess couldn't believe the irony of the situation.

Tom shook his head. 'Jessica, Linda said she's been calling you more often lately because she's been trying to figure out a way to ask for your help. She wants out of your father's games, out of his house, but doesn't know how to do it.'

'What? Then why didn't she say so?'

'Because she doesn't have that kind of open and honest relationship with you. She envies what you and Scott had together.'

'But…' Jess hiccuped a few times and closed her eyes. 'It's all too confusing.' She looked up at him again. 'And you found all this out this evening?'

'Yes. I think, as an outsider, I could see the cry for help more clearly than you.'

'That still doesn't explain why you were kissing her.'

'I didn't kiss her, Jessica,' he explained patiently. 'She kissed me. It was a welcome-to-the-family kiss. Besides, I'd promised to speak to you and offered her any help she might need in leaving the nest, so to speak. No doubt your father will cut her off without a cent.'

'Probably. That'll be hard for Linda to come to terms with.' Jess still wasn't sure she trusted her sister's motives and said so. 'For as long as I can remember, she's manipulated me and everyone else around her—just like our father.'

'I understand your reticence,' Tom remarked. 'But what if she's telling the truth? You've got to give her the benefit of the doubt.'

'Easier said than done. Just don't ever kiss her again,' she warned. 'It's happened to me far too often, Tom.'

'You have my word, Jessica. Linda really isn't my type.'

'So who *is* your type?' She smiled up at him, recalling the question that had started the roller-coaster ride to where they were today.

'You are,' he whispered tenderly, as he urged her closer. His aftershave teased at her senses and Jess groaned with longing. His lips moved over hers with complete familiarity and she kissed him back without reservation.

'Oh, for crying out loud!' a man exclaimed, and Jess's sluggish senses recognised the voice as belonging to her father. She snuggled deeper into Tom's embrace, daring her father to say something.

'Typical behaviour, Jessie. I expected it of you as a teenager, but as an adult?' He shook his head sadly. 'All a father does is try to provide the best for his family—isn't that right, dear?' he asked his wife, who held his hand.

'Save your speeches for the media.' Jess stood and Tom did the same. 'If you're so adamant about doing right for

your family, the first thing you would have done would
have been to ask us about Linda.'

Her father's eyes turned from accusing to piercing in an
instant. The mask had been shed. 'Linda? I presume she's
under someone's care, although why the ambulance had to
bring her to a public hospital is beyond me. We have
enough money to pay for private treatment.'

'Only the best for your little girl, eh?'

'Don't be so impertinent, Jessie. Linda's lucky I don't
cut her off without a cent this very night after what she did
to me. Right in the middle of my speech. She puts on her
display of pain and anguish and then *you…*' Hank stabbed
a finger at Jess. '*You* push your way through the crowd to
get to her instead of staying by Sean's side. Do you have
any idea how bad that's going to look in the photographs
for tomorrow's newspaper?'

Every muscle in Jess's body was clenched tightly, her
eyes wide with horrified amazement at what her father was
saying. She'd forgotten the utter depths of his shallowness
and couldn't believe she was related to him. She glanced
at her mother, who was standing dutifully by his side, fo-
cusing on her perfectly manicured nails.

'I still can't believe Linda did what she did. I mean, what
was she thinking? *You*, sure, I'd expect a stunt like that
from you, but not from Linda. She's always been such a
good girl, always doing as she was told.' He shook his head
as though completely baffled.

'She was in *pain*.' Jess spoke slowly, as though talking
to an imbecile. 'Her reaction was completely involuntary.'

'Oh, nonsense. You can control any kind of pain,' her
father spouted. 'What's the use of having medicine if you
can't control pain? That's what this world lacks—complete
control.'

'And I suppose you're going to guide the sad excuse for
the human race through it?'

'Running for State Premier will certainly be a step in the right direction.'

Jess's anger increased but she felt Tom squeeze her hand. She turned to look at him and he shook his head ever so slightly. Jess got the message.

'Why don't we try and get an update on Linda's condition?' Tom said, and all but tugged Jess out of the room. 'He's not worth it, Jessica,' he said as they headed to the clerk's station. They enquired after Linda and received a reply that she'd be out of Theatre directly.

Tom smiled brightly at the clerk and switched on his natural charm. 'Is there some where else we can wait?'

'Well, as you're both doctors, I guess it would be all right for you to wait in the doctors' lounge,' the clerk told them hesitantly.

'Thank you.' Once they were settled, Jess turned to face Tom.

'Can you see why I didn't want to come?'

'Yes, but you did come, Jessica, and that in itself is to be commended. You were correct in thinking your father might lay a trap for you, and he did. He let you down yet again and that must feel…awful.'

Jess sighed. 'I can't say that's one of the emotions I'm feeling right now because anger is the dominant one. It just strengthens my resolve not have anything to do with them.'

'You shouldn't say that,' Tom reproached softly.

'How can you say that? After everything that's happened tonight, Tom, how can you say that?'

'Because there may come a time, Jessica, when your family might be genuinely reaching out to you—just as Linda is trying to. If you're not there for them…' He shrugged sadly.

Jess felt tears prick behind her eyes. 'They use me every time, Tom.'

'I know, sweetheart. I know,' he murmured, and gathered her into his arms. 'I've lived with resentment ever since I can remember. Resenting my parents, the foster-homes I was in, the police, the system. It eats away at you if you let it.' He pulled back and looked down into her face, kissing away her tears. 'Don't resent your family any more, Jessica. Accept them for who they are—and their power over you will disappear. Accept that your father is first and foremost a politician and everything he does is to further his career. Accept that your mother is a woman who's vowed to support him in any way she can. Accept that Linda wants to change.' He pressed his mouth to her lips, his kiss holding a lasting promise. 'Accept that Scott gave you a wonderful gift,' he said softly. 'The wonderful gift of a true sibling. Someone who cares and shares equally with you. Many people, myself included, never find that, Jessica. Hold onto those memories and don't let the bad ones cloud them.'

Jess choked on the lump in her throat and coughed before burying her face in his shoulder.

'Is everything all right?' someone asked from the doorway, and Jess quickly raised her head, wiping at her eyes. 'I'm Dr Browne.' He came over and shook hands with first Tom and then Jess. 'You're Linda's sister?' he asked, and Jess nodded. 'She's a very lucky girl. The appendix perforated on the table, so thankfully we were able to ensure nothing leaked into the peritoneum. She's in Recovery if you want to see her.'

'Yes. Thank you.'

'I'll go with Dr Browne to tell your parents,' Tom said, and winked at her.

Jess nodded and followed Dr Browne's directions through to Recovery. She stopped at the foot of the bed and looked down at her sister. Her blonde hair was fanned out on the pillow. Even after an operation, she managed to look beautiful. Jess took a deep breath and walked slowly around to the side of the bed. She took Linda's hand in hers and whispered, 'Poor little rich girl.' For the first time in Jess's life, she felt the stirrings of empathy for her sister. A sister who'd been singled out and spoiled.

'Jessie?' Linda's voice croaked.

'I'm here,' Jess replied, and squeezed her sister's hand.

'I thought I was going to die. I was so scared.'

'You're going to be fine.' A tear slid down Jess's cheek.

Linda opened her eyes momentarily and looked at her sister. 'Crying? For me?' Linda closed her eyes again and swallowed, her breath catching in her dry throat, making her cough.

'Here.' Jess spooned some ice chips into Linda's mouth.

'Why the tears?' Linda whispered a moment later. 'I know you don't care about me.'

'That's not true,' Jess replied earnestly.

'No. You cared about Scott and that was all.'

Jess shook her head. When had things become such a mess? 'Scott needed me. You had everyone else.'

'And the only thing I've ever wanted was a relationship like you and Scotty had.' Linda started to cry and Jess dabbed her tears dry with a tissue.

'Shh,' she soothed. 'We can talk about it later.'

'No. Now, Jessie. Why do you think I call you all the time?'

'Because you want my attention.'

'But do I get it?' Linda's words started slurring more than before and Jess knew that part of her sister's emotional outburst was due to the anaesthetic drugs. Then again, the anaesthetic might be the cause of all this honesty.

Jess raked her free hand through her hair. 'Perhaps we need to stop seeing each other as sisters, Linda, and just become friends.'

Linda opened her eyes again. 'How?'

Jess smiled. 'I'll teach you.'

'Yeah.' She closed her eyes. 'Yeah. I'd like that.'

'Give me a call when you're ready and we'll take it from there. For now you need to rest,' Jess said softly, before leaving her sister to sleep off the effects of the anaesthetic. She returned to the family waiting room, only to find her father staring accusingly at Tom, her mother looking bored and Tom casually drinking a cup of coffee.

'Linda's in Recovery and doing just fine,' Jess announced.

'Excellent.' Tom drained his cup and crossed to Jess's side. He placed his arm about her shoulders and kissed her forehead. 'Tell me about it later,' he said softly, and she marvelled at just how well he knew her. Better than anyone else.

'Will you stop all this mushy stuff with my daughter?' her father began. 'Her life now is with—'

Tom held up his hand for silence and amazingly her father stopped speaking. 'Jessica and I are going to leave now. We're returning to your home, getting our bags and heading to the airport.'

'But she's supposed to marry Sean,' her father protested loudly.

'Sorry, Hank, but she's already engaged to someone else.'

'I am?' Jess looked up at him in astonishment. Tom smiled down happily at her and Jess's heart thumped out of control. Remembering who they were with, she turned back to face her parents. 'It appears I'm already spoken for.' She tingled with happiness. 'Thank you for inviting me here this weekend. I've…learnt a lot.'

'Now that we know Linda is out of the woods, my fiancé and I will be leaving. Have a pleasant evening,' Tom said, and before her father could utter another word, he propelled Jess out of the door and out of the hospital.

On the taxi ride back to her parents' house, Tom was quieter than he'd been at the hospital. Jess started to feel a bit nervous. Had he just announced their engagement to protect her? When Dirk Robertson had been bothering her,

Tom had protected her. Was he doing the same now? Protecting her again?

She sneaked a glance at him, only to see him still gazing out into the darkness of the night. Didn't he know she needed to hear some sort of confirmation of his statement? If it *had* been just to protect her, surely he'd say so.

Jess felt her happiness subside as she turned to stare out of the opposite window. A few seconds later, she decided it was pointless to keep fretting about it. 'Tom?' No reply. 'Tom?' she said a bit more forcefully, and he turned quickly to look at her.

'Sorry. I was miles away.' His smile was encompassing, as was his arm, which he placed around her shoulders to draw her closer.

'Take me with you next time, then I won't get so lonely.' The taxi stopped outside her parents' house and, after asking the taxi driver to wait, they rushed inside, changed and packed.

On their way down the corridor, Jess stopped at her old bedroom and slowly pushed open the door. She turned on the light and gazed around the room. 'Just accept,' she said softly, and felt Tom's hand on her shoulder. 'This room was my haven and, although I despised the colour scheme as I got older, it holds a lot of memories.'

'Where's Scott's room?'

Jess laughed sadly and shook her head. 'Further away than the aubergine room. I believe it's now a storage room.'

'You can't know what's going on inside your parents' heads, Jessica. They may still be grieving for Scott, you don't know that. Perhaps keeping busy is the way they cope with it. Don't judge them, honey.'

'You're right.' Jess closed the door to her room and together they headed down the stairs and back into the waiting taxi. When they arrived at the airport, Jess found that Tom had already arranged everything. They were booked on a flight to Sydney where they would stay the night and then return to Adelaide later on Sunday.

'I thought we could do a bit of shopping in Sydney. It's been a while since I've been there,' Tom said as they settled themselves into the business class seats.

Jess looked at him in surprise. 'When did you organise all this?'

'After your father and I had our little…chat. I wasn't taking any chances, Jessica. I wasn't going to leave you behind. Your father only spoke to me for about five minutes and after he'd ranted and raved about how I was an inconsequential specimen of the human race who would never be permitted to marry his oldest daughter, I was left alone.'

'But when I came back into the ballroom, you were with Linda.'

He nodded. 'She came in about ten minutes after your father had left.' He shook his head. 'She didn't look too well then. Why didn't I pick it up?'

'Don't blame yourself, Tom. Linda was in denial of any pain and had you questioned her, she would have downplayed any symptoms.'

'At least she received prompt medical attention.'

'At least.' The plane taxied along the runway then rose into the air. They talked about a variety of topics as they were served their refreshments and settled down to watch a movie. All the while, Jess wanted to ask Tom about his engagement comment. Usually, she had no problem with taking the bull by the horns, but in this instance, if Tom were to say it *had* only been to protect her against her father, she wanted to live with the dream for a little bit longer. After all, she loved him.

Twice more she caught him staring out the window into the blackness of the night. Eventually, Jess decided she *needed* to know the truth. 'Tom?'

'Mmm?' He slowly turned to face her. 'What's up?'

Jess opened her mouth but closed it quickly. She took a

deep breath and tried again. 'When you…you know, told my parents we were…' She faltered and looked down at her clenched hands.

'Engaged?' he supplied.

'Yes. Well…were you just protecting me?'

'Yes.'

Jess hung her head and closed her eyes, trying desperately to hide her pain at his answer. She felt the tears gathering and willed them to stop—but they wouldn't. She pursed her lips together and sniffed.

'Jessica. Jessica, look at me.' He placed his hand beneath her chin and edged her head up. He dabbed at her eyes with a handkerchief and smiled at her. 'Jessica,' he said when she opened her eyes, 'of course I was protecting you. It's a primal instinct in a man to protect the woman he loves.'

'What?' She frowned at him before blowing her nose. 'What?'

Tom cupped her face in his hands. 'Jessica, I love you.' He laughed. 'Wow. That was easier to say than I'd anticipated.' He pressed his lips to hers before holding her tightly. 'You're so absolutely perfect for me,' he said as he rested his forehead against hers. 'I never thought I'd find you, and now that I have I'm never letting you go.' Tom kissed her again before drawing back to gaze into her eyes. 'Jessica, will you do me the honour of becoming my wife?'

Tears started to flood down Jess's cheeks and she smiled at him. 'Oh, Tom,' she sobbed. 'Yes. Yes.' She started to laugh. 'Oh, Tom,' she said again, and pressed her lips to his. When they broke apart, she dabbed at her eyes and blew her nose again. 'This day has been…'

'Exhausting,' he said with a nod. 'But in a good way. When you told me that you loved me, it was as though you'd given me the most precious gift in the world. Indeed, you *have* given it to me but, to be honest, Jessica, I wasn't quite sure what to do with it. I knew my feelings for you

ran deep—deeper than I've ever felt for any other woman—
but was that going to be enough?'

'What happened?'

'Your father. He'd probably twist his intestines into a
hernia if he knew he was the source of clarifying my true
feelings for you.' Tom chuckled. 'I was amazed at his pre-
sumption in deciding what was best for your life, and it
drove home to me that you were suited to no one else but
me. I'm your soul-mate, Jessica, and neither your father
nor anyone else was going to stop me from spending the
rest of my life with you.'

'But…in the taxi and just before…you were so quiet, so
withdrawn. I felt for certain that you were trying to figure
out a way to tell me our engagement wasn't real.'

'On the contrary.' Tom smiled adoringly at her. 'I was
trying to get up the nerve to tell you how much I loved
you. How I want us to be together…for as long as we both
shall live.' With that, Tom pressed his lips against hers,
carrying an eternal promise of love.

'Tom,' she breathed when they finally broke apart. 'You
make me so very happy.' Jess chuckled to herself.

'What are you laughing at?'

'For years, Tom, I've moved from one place to another.
First to hide from my family and then to hide from myself.
If I stayed in one place for too long I started to become
attached to things.'

'Is this also why you don't have any furniture?'

Jess laughed again. 'Probably.'

'So what about now? Do you still want to keep moving,
Jessica?' The joviality was gone from his tone and Jess felt
her own smile disappear.

'I may move again—some time in the future—but for
the next four months I need to concentrate on finishing my
registrar training. After that, though, I only want to move
to wherever you are.' She kissed him. 'The moving was a

way of finding out where I really belonged. Now I *know* where I belong. I belong with you.'

'Yes, you do,' he agreed, 'and I'm looking forward to our life together—but there's one request I need to make.'

'What is it?' Jess was instantly alert.

'After we're married, *please*, can we get rid of your futon and buy a proper bed? I don't think my aging joints can handle it.'

Jess laughed and hugged him. 'Of course. Shall we seal it with a kiss?'

'Jessica, darling, I thought you'd never ask.'

EPILOGUE

'CLOSE your eyes,' Jess heard Tom whisper from behind her. He stood with one possessive arm about her, the other cradling their two month old son, Christopher.

'Are her eyes *really* closed?' Harley asked. 'I think she's peeking, Tom.'

'They're closed,' Jess answered, her excitement turning to impatience. 'When are you going to tell me what's going on?' she demanded, giving her husband a playful nudge with her elbow. He didn't answer. She listened carefully, hearing scuffling noises.

'All right,' Tom said a few seconds later. 'Open your eyes.'

'Surprise!' Everyone chorused.

'What?' Jess's eyes scanned the large family room of the home she and Tom had moved into after their wedding. The room that had been empty a few minutes ago was now filled with people. People Tom and Jess called family.

Clarissa, Nicola and their respective families were all beaming brightly at them. Betty and her husband. Kathryn and Jack. Everyone who was dear to them. Jess felt tears prick—tears of happiness.

'I...I...don't know what to say,' she spluttered laughingly.

'Say, ''Harley and Tom, how did you do it?''' Harley prompted. Jess gazed lovingly at the teenager and held out her hand to him. He came over willingly and she marvelled at the difference a year of living in a happy, healthy environment had made on him. Once he'd recovered from his accident, he'd fled the foster-home and after returning from their honeymoon, Jess and Tom had taken him in. Tom was the only person in the world the young boy had respected and slowly, over the course of time, he'd come to respect her as well.

'How did you do it?' she repeated obligingly.

'It *wasn't* easy,' he groaned. He almost equalled her in height and as he was now sixteen and still growing, she was interested to see if he'd top Tom!

'Ready for your next surprise?' Tom asked as he kissed her cheek.

'What? There's more?' As she spoke, the lights went out and for a second she thought there'd been a power failure. Christopher gurgled happily, unperturbed by the goings-on around him, and Jess's heart turned over with love for her son.

Candlelight flickered in the doorway and Jess looked over to see Linda and Sean carrying in a large rectangular cake with the words, HAPPY 1ST WEDDING ANNIVERSARY on it. People starting singing 'Happy Anniversary' to the tune of 'Happy Birthday' and all Jess could do was openly gape at the sight of her sister.

Linda, with Sean's help, placed the cake on the table before crossing to her sister's side. 'Surprised?' she asked with a laugh.

'Very! What are you two doing here?' Jess kissed her sister and then Sean. 'I spoke to you yesterday,' she accused Linda. 'And you never said a word!'

'Your husband would have disowned us,' Sean replied.

'Are Mum and Dad here, too?' Jess asked hopefully.

'No.' Linda's tone was soft and apologetic. 'Dad's swamped with work but they did send a gift for Christopher.'

'They're going to spoil him rotten.' Jess looked at her son who still had the same hypnotic blue eyes as his father. The same nose and the same encompassing smile. 'Then again, I don't blame them one little bit.'

'Aw, come on,' Harley groaned as he walked over to the stereo. 'This is supposed to be a party!'

'Not too loud,' Tom called. 'Or you'll be the one getting up for Christopher tonight.'

As people started to dance, Tom handed his son over to his very clucky aunt and took Jess in his arms.

'Happy anniversary, Mrs Bryant,' he murmured next to her ear.

'Thank you.' Jess sighed into the embrace of the man she loved and adored. The man who had taught her how to accept people and to love them unconditionally. The man who had supported her through her final exams and who had celebrated with her when she'd qualified.

Never in her life had she received such support or love from anyone as she did from Tom and she had the perfect gift to give him on this, their first wedding anniversary.

'If you don't mind, I'd like to give you your present in private,' she whispered as she drew him closer. She kissed his lips seductively.

'Now, now,' he said with frustration as he tried to pull back slightly. 'Not until you've had the all-clear from the doctor. Christopher's only eight weeks old and your delivery wasn't the easiest in the world.'

'Oh, you're so gorgeous,' she told him, remembering how he'd been so comforting during her difficult delivery. Jess kissed him again. 'I saw the doctor today,' she whispered in his ear. 'I've been given the all-clear.'

Tom jerked back to look at her, his blue eyes smouldering with barely repressed desire.

'Surprise!' She laughed and he groaned, resting his head on her shoulder. 'Now all you have to do is wait for everyone to leave and for Christopher to stay asleep.'

He raised his head and kissed her—deeply, passionately, wildly.

'I look forward to it, Mrs Bryant. I look forward to it!'

Modern Romance™
...seduction and
passion guaranteed

Tender Romance™
...love affairs that
last a lifetime

Sensual Romance™
...sassy, sexy and
seductive

Blaze
...sultry days and
steamy nights

Medical Romance™
...medical drama on
the pulse

Historical Romance™
...rich, vivid and
passionate

27 new titles every month.

*With all kinds of Romance for
every kind of mood...*

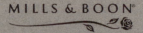

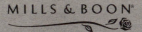

Medical Romance™

A DOCTOR'S COURAGE *by Gill Sanderson*

The new GP in her country practice is unlike any man
District Nurse Nikki Gale has met before. The more
she gets to know Dr Tom Murray, the more she
wants him. Tom's prognosis for the future is
uncertain, but Nikki is determined to show him he
doesn't have to face his fears alone.

THE NURSE'S SECRET CHILD *by Sheila Danton*

Though Max and Jenny had a passionate relationship,
marriage and children had never featured in their
future plans. Only Jenny became pregnant – and
before she could tell Max she discovered he had
always intended to marry someone else. Four years
on, Max is back – as a consultant in her hospital! And
now she has to decide how to tell Max about her
secret.

THE FATHER OF HER BABY *by Joanna Neil*

It had been a struggle, but Bethany wouldn't change a
thing about her life. She has a rewarding job as a GP
and an adorable son, Sam. But now Connor
Broughton was back in town. Should she tell him
about her baby? In the end he found out on his own –
and asked the one question she didn't want to answer:
who was Sam's father?

On sale 6th September 2002

2 Books
and a surprise gift!

We would like to take this opportunity to thank you for reading this Mills & Boon® book by offering you the chance to take TWO more specially selected titles from the Medical Romance™ series absolutely FREE! We're also making this offer to introduce you to the benefits of the Reader Service™ —

* ★ FREE home delivery
* ★ FREE gifts and competitions
* ★ FREE monthly Newsletter
* ★ Books available before they're in the shops
* ★ Exclusive Reader Service discount

Accepting these FREE books and gift places you under no obligation to buy; you may cancel at any time, even after receiving your free shipment. Simply complete your details below and return the entire page to the address below. *You don't even need a stamp!*

YES! Please send me 2 free Medical Romance books and a surprise gift. I understand that unless you hear from me, I will receive 4 superb new titles every month for just £2.55 each, postage and packing free. I am under no obligation to purchase any books and may cancel my subscription at any time. The free books and gift will be mine to keep in any case.

M2ZEB

Ms/Mrs/Miss/Mr ....Initials...
BLOCK CAPITALS PLEASE

Surname..

Address..

....

....Postcode ....

Send this whole page to:
UK: The Reader Service, FREEPOST CN81, Croydon, CR9 3WZ
EIRE: The Reader Service, PO Box 4546, Kilcock, County Kildare (stamp required)

Offer not valid to current Reader Service subscribers to this series. We reserve the right to refuse an application and applicants must be aged 18 years or over. Only one application per household. Terms and prices subject to change without notice. Offer expires 29th November 2002. As a result of this application, you may receive offers from other carefully selected companies. If you would prefer not to share in this opportunity please write to The Data Manager at the address above.

Mills & Boon® is a registered trademark owned by Harlequin Mills & Boon Limited.
Medical Romance ™ is being used as a trademark.